The Generalist
Taboo 0: Cliché of Memories
by Thomas Duder

This is a work of fiction, despite what Thomas Duder claims.
All the characters and events portrayed in this book are either products of the author's imagination or are used fictitiously. This is a work of fiction based on events true or real, but only with express permission from those individuals. All others named are purely coincidental. All well-known pop culture references, memes, lyrics and song titles are used only as either a homage or gentle parody.
All rights reserved. Any reproduction in any media of the content and/or images used in this book without written permission from the publisher is a violation of copyright law.

ISBN-13: 978-1480196285
ISBN-10: 1480196282

Published by
Massive Entertainment
P.O. Box 30462
Bellingham, WA 98228

Published through Amazon's Createspace Engine

The Generalist - Taboo 0: Cliché of Memories. Copyright ©2012 by Thomas Duder. All rights reserved.
The Generalist - Taboo 0: Cliché of Memories. Edited by Adele Symonds. Copyright ©2013 by Adele Symonds and Thomas Duder. All rights reserved.

The Generalist - Taboo 0: Cliché of Memories jacket cover. Copyright ©2012 by Jade Flores and Thomas Duder. All rights reserved.
Visit Jade and the rest of her wonderful work at
http://jadedshots.blogspot.com
To visit Ace and see the man behind the troll, check out
http://dangercombo2012.blogspot.com
Meet the real Vorel Kethend at
http://modelingintherain.blogspot.com
Check out Adele Symond's other works at
http://www.adelesymondscom
For the latest from Thomas Duder, visit any of his nine blogs at either The Pen Is My Sword (http://www.thepenismysword.com) or That Bastard On... (http://on.thepenismysword.com), or visit the Hooligans at either Nerf All The Things (http://www.nerfallthethings.com) or KAOS: Chaos Party Radio (http://www.kaosparty.com)!
Come check out "Da Hooliganz" at either KAOS: Chaos Party Radio, at Blazin' Ace's site
http://www.youtube.com/BlazingAceNelson or at their own site at http://www.youtube.com/TheDamnHooligans

WARNING!

The Generalist novella series contains the following – serious violence, religious issues, some scenes of a sensual nature, and "alternative lifestyle arrangements." If you aren't into that, this probably isn't the kind of series for you.

If it is, then enjoy!
If it ain't, you may kindly stop readin' here and take the time to de-ass the situation.

More from Thomas Duder...

The Generalist

Taboo 0 - Cliché of Memories -

Taboo 1 – Where's The Beef?

Taboo 2 – Magic and Mayhem (Part 1 of The Mayhem Arc)

Taboo 3 – Misfits and Mayhem (Part 2 of The Mayhem Arc)

Omnibus – Volume 1 (WIP)

Taboo 4 – Angle of the Angels (WIP)

Killer 13 (WIP)

I

II

III

IV

V

VI

VII

CHOOSE YOUR DESTINY

From The Author..1
Round 1..5
Round 2..19
Round 3..36
Round 4..60
Round 5..84
And now for a preview of
The Generalist – Taboo 1: Where's the Beef?..................97

****

The Generalist
From The Author

In through the nose.

Count to ten.

Out through the mouth.

Count to ten.

I keep doing this, but no matter how many times I do it I keep finding my eyes drawn to the physical copy, sure just a proof but still...physical nonetheless. I then find myself touching the damn thing, reading it. Realizing that it's real.

Sure I curse the fact that the back image is missing the unhappy face logo, or that Round 1 apparently has the title wrong for some reason...but still.

But STILL....

It's my book. My pride and joy, my hard work, sweat, and tears given form.

My autobiography, of sorts, my words....all these characters, this world I've created.

It's all right here. I'm holding it now, even as we speak. It's on my lap as I type, on my desk while I'm at work, and

Taboo 0: Cliché of Memories

I've taken it everywhere with me. Hell, I've even slept with the thing.

In through the nose....count to ten.

I keep proving to myself that it's real, that it exists, that this physical copy is here...that I myself inhaled the delectable, exquisite aroma of fresh ink and new book as I opened it up. I know it exists, my friends have touched it, held it, seen it for themselves. We've taken pictures with it, Vorel Kethend herself has modeled a few poses with it and Jade (the cover artist) thinks it looks snazzy as hell.

Yet....

Out through the mouth...count to ten.

I have wanted very few things with all my heart, O Dear Reader of mine, ever present and eternal, quiet yet with thoughts so loud that they crash against me. I have ever dared to truly dream yet to achieve something that seems so...unobtainable...

Definitely intangible, in the very least.

This isn't the same as seeing it in e-copy. This is the most primal and greatest joy I have ever known as a reader and...yeah, perhaps also as a writer.

This is as wonderful as hearing the music I've written

The Generalist

played by a band. There is, literally, no joy that I can verbally express that encompasses what I felt as I opened the box and saw my novella, all 100 and some-odd pages of it.

So small, yet so fragile. Something I've directly created brought to life and in my hands, begging me to open it.

Then I flip it over to see the rest of the cover...and the Mean Unhappy Face logo isn't there, faded in the background behind the words.

Well, even flawed as it is, this physical proof copy is still the best benchmark for me as a writer and will give way to a greater degree of a perfected copy afterwards.

You'll see~!

Speakin' about e-copy, you DO realize you can catch most of my stuff for free over at The Pen Is My Sword? I've also got a Author Page that I humbly (yet loudly) invite you to go check out and like. By all means, c'mon over and get yourself some laughs, some crude and offensive material as well as giveaways and generally bullshit around with me and my idjit friends as well as get in on the latest of my stuff, including the wonderful anthologies I'm taking part in.

'Cuz it's always fun 'til someone gets skullfucked.

Taboo 0: Cliché of Memories
The Pen Is My Sword

http://www.thepenismysword.com

Thomas Duder's Author Page

http://www.facebook.com/AuthorOfTheThings

Well. Be seein' ya next time, yah?

Sincerely,

~Thomas Duder, Author Of The Things

P.S. - Yes. *All* of them. All the things.

The Generalist
Round 1

In all the annals of history, in all the eras and ages that have ever passed, there are quite a few generalizations concerning humanity.

One of those is that you are bound to have a truly, terribly bad day when the first thing that happens is that you awaken in a bathtub full of blood.

By you, I mean me.

By bathtub filled with blood, I mean bathtub filled with blood and, well...myself, all Mister Big Naked style.

I kept acting like I was asleep, keeping my breathing deep and my eyes moving as if they were in REM sleep. I "stirred" a bit then pretended to go back to sleep, my eyelids barely opened to allow a thin sliver of light to shatter the darkness. My eyes moving quickly as they were, I was able to take in the scene quickly: the bathtub itself was huge, apparently copper. It stood in the middle of the bathroom like a squatting gargoyle, the bathroom itself reeking of opulence. The checkerboard-patterned tile was rank with ivory and ebony, an entire wall of the bathroom was one humongous, spotlessly clean mirror and, y'know, those his-and-her sinks some people have? Yeah, there was one right next to the doorway leading out. Absolutely nothing on the east and western walls, and

Taboo 0: Cliché of Memories
what walls I COULD see were of the purest marble.

Situation, check. My body felt fine, my mind felt empty and I couldn't remember who the hell I was. I somehow knew (without even knowing how I knew, I just...y'know, *knew*) the price range of the room I was in and yet it didn't feel like mine...nor did I, once again I should point out, know how I knew.

Great. Amnesia. I can only hope that my past self was as snarky as I apparently am.

With no one else in the room and no cameras in sight, I slowly edged my way up to a sitting position and verified what I had quietly sensed earlier: no wounds on my body, so all this blood CERTAINLY couldn't be mine.

Strangely enough it didn't make me feel any better.

Getting out and slipping about a little, I was able to find clean towels, rags, and what appeared to be clothes that fit me. I filled up the 'his' sink with hot water and rinsed off with the 'hers' sink (why did I find that funny?). Ignoring the coffee mug filled to the brim with delicious-smelling, steaming-hot coffee on the sink, I dressed quickly and took a moment to check myself in the mirror while picking out my small, well-kept afro with an eight-pronged plastic, black pick I found in one of the khaki's pockets, taking further stock of myself. Wide shoulders, caramel brown skin, chocolate brown eyes - not exactly a

The Generalist

looker, but darkly handsome. Somewhat full lips, black mutton chops and the black afro spoke of African descent, but the light skin coloration and those cheekbones bespoke of something Caucasian-ish. Besides, I hadn't a clue what racial grouping begat that somewhat raccoon-esque coloration around the eyes themselves, the sockets made slightly darker due to the long, straight bangs that flowed over them, covering them in shadow whenever I moved my head. Tucking the bangs behind an ear and out of my sight, I ran a hand through the pockets of the black khakis I wore and realized what felt wrong.

Untucking and unbuttoning the black button-up shirt, no design on it nor label on the collar (snazzy~!) and letting it hang, I noted that wearing it like that felt a bit better, certainly something my body was used to. The various assortment of cheap knives, rocks, and vials of liquid in my abnormally deep pants pockets didn't feel any better to me, poking me through the pockets as they were, but I resisted the initial urge to get rid of them - something within me told me that I might have use for such objects. What struck me as strangest was the absolute lack of any cards with a name on it – instead I found a small silver flask with ornate, Gothic writing in some script I didn't recognize that went back into my rear left pocket. For a second it felt warm and I realized I couldn't feel it anymore while it was IN the pocket, but the moment I reached for it - boom, there it was, a nice bulge in the back pocket until I took my hand away and it disappeared

Taboo 0: Cliché of Memories

again.

Well, at least it wasn't uncomfortable. Weird, but there was a strange comfort knowing I could sit down without busting a back pocket with the damn thing.

Lacing up and stomping about in the heavy, steel-toed boots I stopped to check myself in that mirror again.

Yeah, lookin' good. Now I just need to figure out more of my situation.

Indeed, I answered myself, we really DO need to find out what's going on here. Bathtub full of blood, these clothes just layin' in a pile but my stuff unransacked? Someone put me in here for some reason, and I need to go get answers.

"Well, where do YOU normally go to get answers," I asked myself.

"...the Yellow Pages! that second voice answered back, *at least that feels like what we'd've done. Right?"*

I stopped for a moment and thought hard on that, then asked, *"You're just the voice in my head, right?"*

" Well, yeah...at least I am, yeah? I mean, you're you and I'm me. I'm you, and you're me...but I can't be you, and you can't be me, right?"

The Generalist

My head hurt at the so-called logic of that response and after putting an ear to the door and listening out for strangers, I eased the door open as soundlessly as I could and slid into the rest of the place, intent on getting the hell outta Dodge and back into whatever might jog my memory back. In the very least, get into a more comfortable position than where I currently found myself.

*****

Despite the disgusting expensiveness of the condo, as richly furnished as the bathroom had been and just as upper-class gauche, the rest of the neighborhood quickly fell from upper-crust condos and suburbs into the strangely comforting nitty-gritty of the darker aspects of the city. Graffiti dotted the buildings here and there, and low-rent apartments and mini-marts lay jam-packed alongside brick buildings and gas stations.

"So all I'm saying is that it's funny that we've come across, what, five different phone booths with no Yellow Pages, even back in the affluent part of town, y'know?" Said the voice in my head, by now having given me a steady stream of chatter to take my mind off my slightly depressing situation, *"I mean here we are, puttin' feet to the street, yeah? At least THAT much feels familiar! Hey, do you remember anything yet? 'Cuz I don't remember*

Taboo 0: Cliché of Memories

much right now."

Earlier I had mentally yelled at the Voice to shut up already, only to practically feel it sulk and mope in the darkness of my headspace. Deciding that I'd rather have the Voice cheerfully talk to me while being alone within the small crowd that journeyed on the sidewalk of the city, I told it to talk again and apologized.

Then it wouldn't shut up again. I have a feeling that this has happened to me before, but it was better that at least one of us was cheerful, so much so that I stopped caring that I might be a schizophrenic suffering from multiple personality disorder as well as being an amnesiac.

All the smells and sounds of the inner city assaulted me, and the myriad of its denizens moving here and there on their own business - all this felt a bit more comfortable to me than the situation I woke up in, and I was strangely happy at seeing the dilapidated streets and lost souls walking about the way I was, intent on their late-evening travels and ignoring that anyone else existed. Some cared only of the bad day they'd had, others thought of the usual litany of the human condition: food, sex, money. Desire, greed, lust. Love. Hate. Happiness. Anger.

For whatever reason, all their emotions flowed through me and into me, calming me with the strange music that the city represented to me...or at least I should have been

The Generalist

calmed – I instinctively knew I should've been by now, that I did this on a regular basis.

Except I was being followed currently, and had been followed for the past ten minutes or so. That shit pissed me right off.

Passing by a basketball court with a chain link fence, I hauled myself to the side and ducked down an alleyway, wanting to face whomever was following me in a battlefield of my choosing. The alleyway itself emptied out to the other side, and except for a dumpster it was big enough that I'd have room to maneuver (woah, I knew Kung Fu! Well, some kind of fighting art - I could feel my body relax and prepare for the fight) yet there wasn't enough room for me to be easily surrounded.

To my relief (and the relief of my Voice) there was only one guy. To our mutual horror it was a huge creature with red glowing eyes that panted and growled at the end of the alleyway, glaring at me and flexing its humongous claws, obviously taller and bulkier than me, wearing a beige trench coat and a fisherman's hat of equal color.

Green skin, ginormous legs and arms, a strangely thin trunk in comparison to those limbs and his flexing, giant, scaly fingers were tipped with excruciatingly noticeable claws that glinted in the murky streetlight of the alley. How did this thing move about normal society without

Taboo 0: Cliché of Memories

being spotted? It sure as hell scared me, and scared me further still as it panted and growled, glaring at me the entire time, flexing those frightening claws and trembling with what could only be described as tangible rage.

"Frank. Todd," the creature panted, its eyes still glowing red, like pissed-off laser lights, from under its greenish-black hair. Was it wearing armor under that huge trench coat? Hell, it was wearing pants, camouflage-colored baggy khakis!

"FRANK! TODD!!!!" the creature roared, beginning to lumber towards me, its face a twisted visage of pure mad. Not, like, normal mad but someone-threw-a-folding-chair mad.

"What should we do?!" I asked my Voice in a mental tone that was way calmer than I felt. The animal instinct part of my mind gibbered and growled, trying to make sense as the creature drew closer: it was certainly humanoid, but those arms...those hands! My, grandmaw, what big nails you have!

"I already ran, except I'm in your head," The Voice, who was currently the smartest guy in my head, screamed back at me, *"Run! RUN!"*

And so I did.

Something screamed and I realized it was me,

The Generalist

screaming like a damn fool with my hands over my ears as I hauled ass to the other side of the alleyway, intent on putting distance between me and the...the...shit, it was a monster. It was a freaking monster!

Ignoring the roared cries of the monstrosity I hauled harder, wanting to get away, wanting to get AWAY! From those claws, those glaring red eyes, the rows of sharp teeth it had.

I didn't want to think about it, I only wanted to get away from it, and I did just that. By the time I turned around to see that there was no one left on the street I realized several things.

I was panting, standing and looking around like a fool in the middle of the street. I had lost the monster. I had also run insanely hard and was now in yet another part of the city, a school to my left and an overpass to my right. Looking up, I forced myself to regulate my breathing and take another stab at locating where I was and figuring out where I needed to go from there.

I had outrun the monster, but ohhhhh baby...this night was just getting better and better.

****

Taboo 0: Cliché of Memories

Picking the lock to the elementary school was easy at this time of night, and I finally got a chance to get a better idea of what was going on. It was 10 p.m. on a Friday night according to the principal's computer, and I was in (New) Los Angeles. As I checked around the internet, I felt superficial information and memories return - I still didn't know quite who I was beyond my name, but I at least knew what the year and date today was and where I was (James Woods Memorial Elementary), then I ran a check for my name. Not too many with that specific combination of names, and at the very least I could ascertain whether or not I was a sex offender (amongst other things).

Gaining food and FINALLY finding a Yellow Pages, I began to scan about for anything that would stand out to me, flipping through the book swiftly, my eyes scanning quickly, whilst wolfing down the two loaded hot dogs carefully - no need to get ketchup and onions all over the place, y'know?

"So how DO you know how to do all this stuff anyway?" my annoying Voice asked me.

That one stopped me cold - picking the lock could possibly point towards me being a criminal (ergo my search for my name in certain criminal databases), and for some strange reason I could see myself as a sexual deviant. Hopefully not TOO deviant though, I might not

The Generalist

like myself afterwards.

"I dunno," I answered back honestly, *"Brute hacking passwords are easy, at least it feels easy. Ditching and dodging the security cams were also easy. Hitting up these databases won't show much, though it'll show snoops and earworm programs that SOMEONE here looked up Frank Todd, tipping off their masters to unnatural activity. At this point in time, I'll be happy with...nyoho, hello!"*

Franklin Theodore Todd. I'm, apparently, a bad man.

A very, very bad man.

The list of jobs and skills the FBI (don't ask - I don't remember how I know these passwords, but I remember them) has on my file reads like a bad fan-fiction. The groups and organizations that are connected to me are...well, let's just say they're freakin' impressive. The whole thing is startin' to make me feel like I'm in a bad John Grisham novel, and even at his best the protagonists usually get fucked over and out.

I'm associated with the Catholic Church, the Rosicrucians (*the Order of the Rosy Cross*, an interestin' name my Voice plucks out of the ethers of our...my...brain), some family by the name of Scarletti, and some weird Japanese name I can't even read right now. I don't have a criminal record apparently, but there's more than a few red x's in official lookin' boxes with

Taboo 0: Cliché of Memories

nothing next to them, and obvious redactions like that worries the unholy fuck out of me.

I'm completely flabbergasted when I reach my previous employment section.

Martial arts instructor. Wrestling instructor. Detective. Chemist. Alchemist. Plumber. Electrician. Mechanic. Scientist. Astrophysicist. Mage. Physiologist. Historian. Artificer. Esper. Writer. Duelist – Swordsman. Marksman. Loan shark. Knee-capper. Bouncer.

Exorcist. Banisher. Onmyoji Mystic. Bushiden.

"Generalist." They're calling me a Generalist. I see why.

What the hell though...Alchemist? Scientist? Scientist of what? Esper? Artificer? I can't even SPELL those, let alone understand what the hell they are and how I became them.

Don't even get me started on the entire line from "Exorcist" to "Bushiden."

"Gesundheit," my Voice said.

"Shut up," I replied.

Next to each title, I saw full licenses and degrees of various kinds, and for the more outlandish titles there were only names, presumably of those who trained me.

The Generalist

Now, all this doesn't weird me out nearly as much as the fact that there are several notes that state that I'm under house arrest, as well as complaints from agents that they either can't make it stick or can't find me from time to time.

Interestin'.

This doesn't explain everything, but I'm already startin' to get an idea in my head as to what might've happened to me, or at least why. Nice people don't wake up in empty condo's in bathtubs full of blood with heads lacking memories. Nice people don't have FBI files with notes like "terminate if he exceeds level 5 protocols" or whatever-have-you.

Nice people don't learn this much garbage then NOT work for the good guys, right? Good guys aren't under house arrest and know how to pick locks and hack databases and have confidential, sensitive passwords memorized.

So either I really am out of my mind, monkey nuts, or the world really might be out to get me.

****

Leaps of logic aren't like leaps of faith - for one thing,

Taboo 0: Cliché of Memories

I'm fairly good at the former and completely horrible at the latter. It seemed only natural to look up my name on various databases in order to figure out, at least superficially, who I was. On the other hand, I thought it was a good idea to find the place they had as my last known address and hope for the best that there was more there to remind me of who I was, what I really was, and why I've ended up the way I have - bathtub full of blood, running away from monsters, things like that.

What I got was a small two-story warehouse-like structure, sandwiched between two similar ones. Pure brick, iron shutters, barbed wire around the doorframes, a real character of a place. Above the single door hung a neon blue sign, "The Shop."

Hell, the FBI called it "The Shop" as well. I'm startin' to get a better angle on what kind of guy I was already - all those complicated titles, yet it seems like my thing was more about keeping it simple than anything else.

Approaching the door, I felt something itch at the peripherals of my vision but for the life of me I didn't actively see anything. The Voice in my head felt a little nervous as well, but as we approached the closed door nothing happened. Either we dodged a bullet or just grew accustomed to the place.

After feeling like an idiot to find that the heavy iron

The Generalist

door was obviously locked (fairly obvious, I'm certain I'm the paranoid type even what with all those professions and skills and such) I began to search around for a key and, indeed, I found a heavy key of cold iron underneath the so-called welcome mat.

Go away the welcome mat screamed at me, simple red lettering on a black field.

Yeah, real nice.

That strange, itchy feeling overcame me as I unlocked the door and stepped into a world I simply wasn't expecting.

****

Taboo 0: Cliché of Memories
Round 2

The Shop. A rush of memories came back to me and I remembered this place completely. My threshold, the natural spiritual defenses of a home and my own automated psionic defenses - shit, I was an empath! I fed on and was strengthened by the emotions of others as well as my own, and the training I received from my parents and the Army ensured that my other latent psychic skills were of a useable level.

Esper. The shortened name for "E.S.P. User," and that's one mystery down. While I remembered the rest of The Shop, some of it was still indecipherable to me. Where I stood, for instance, in a room clearly made to appear like a waiting lounge, complete with a secretary's desk at the end of the white padded room. A door led further into The Shop, behind the desk was a filing cabinet, and the two walls (not too far off from where I stood) were lined with comfortably padded, chestnut-colored chairs.

My Voice, for once quiet, felt happy and comfortable for the first time since we woke up and I realized that this was truly home to us, this reception room gave me the feeling that this kind of look apparently appealed to me before my memory loss.

This. A madhouse crossed with a high-rise office.

The Generalist

Heading beyond the door brought me into the rest of The Shop, the first level available to anyone who was able to get past whomever staffed the Welcome Room. Here it looked like an open-air warehouse, separated as it was by various paraphernalia that represented what the section was for - in the far back, behind a wall of small, carefully-tended trees was the herbalist section of the warehouse, resplendent with tables covered with potted plants, full-blown trees (wait, was there DIRT there? Like, the ground underneath the concrete? Did it go through the foundation? How the hell did that work?) growing out of the ground, and a mini-greenhouse with what appeared to be stranger vegetation beyond its cloudy windows. Next to that was a section that was a small maze made by the bookshelves themselves, and I knew there were more comfortable chairs strewn about the maze as well as an inner sanctum area with more chairs and my favorite books. I had spent a lot of time there, and I could practically feel the love radiate from that library.

In the front half of the Shop, closest to the Welcome Room and to either side of me, lay row after row of black shelving with red, mystical inscriptions along the sides that glowed as I drew closer to them. On the rows of shelves lay what I could only guess was random garbage and strange-smelling powders, objects d'art, and random knick-knacks. Wrinkling my nose at the smell of a glowing, green-stoppered test tube I turned from that row and looked down the clean aisleway made by the shelving

Taboo 0: Cliché of Memories

units and whistled in appreciation. Though the shelves were filled with as random a bunch of garbage as I'd ever seen (ornate chests, huge locks, all forms of containers holding powders, salves, oils, rocks and more), it was that strange writing that truly drew me - whenever I got closer to a row of shelves, the writing glowed, re-assembled itself from the chicken-scratch writing to something in English. So many rows though! Were there this many rows when I first got here?

I could hear my Voice mumbling to itself as I passed by each long row of shelving units, *"Unicorn horn. Powdered toast. Virgin's tears. Celebrity dignity. Bones of an honest politician. Frank, what IS all this garbage?"*

"I dunno," I told my Voice, *"But it definitely feels like I've been here before. I'm fairly certain if we keep going down this end of the aisles we'll come across a chemical-mixing room - ayup, there it is!"*

Though I'd been walking far longer than I thought I should (weren't there only a few rows of these racks?) I did indeed eventually come across a partitioned-off room with a door and a humongous window that showcased shiny, cared-for objects of scientific research, expensive-lookin' computer, Bunsen burners, beakers, all kinds of glass containers and vials and measuring tools both arcane and modern.

The Generalist

Looking back, I realized that even though I had been walking for more than a few minutes (even WITH the rubbernecking), there were only a few rows of those shelving units that I had apparently passed, even though my Voice had counted up over twenty we had passed by.

Yet as I looked back, there were only a few rows I had passed by!

"Yeah, definitely not Kansas or anywhere south of the Mason-Dixon Line anymore," I thought to myself.

"Dude, perhaps we should go upstairs?" My Voice suggested.

With that in mind, I headed through the rows of shelving units intent on making for the main clearing area that would take me from this section of the warehouse, through the Library Maze and Herbalist Shop (so many herbs and greenery...was I really a gardening type?) and to the stairs in the back that would lead me to the second floor. Though I noticed an elevator next to the stairs, it didn't feel very me-ish at all: from what I've seen of myself thus far, I was certain the elevator was either shut off, booby-trapped, or somehow would trigger yet another hidden mechanism of some sort. Heading up the stairs, intent on the second floor so high above my head, I noted the mezzanine above the Welcome Room door and realized what was so weird about this structure from the

Taboo 0: Cliché of Memories

get-go.

This wasn't just the one building, it was probably the two adjacent ones as well! I had noted closed signs on them, but now it made a bit more sense as to why there was so much room here. I wondered briefly at what lay at the opposite end of the warehouse on the other side of the shelving units, spying a cook pot of some sort and chalk drawings but by then I had entered the second level of the place.

As expansive and strange as the first level was, the second level was obviously made for living in. There were only the four walls of the Shop warehouse itself, and the rest...well, everything was in its place at least! The kitchen, at the opposite end of the living space in a large corner area, was separated off by an island that held both an oven, stove, and dishwasher with sink segment. From what I could see I had a few modern conveniences but otherwise saw nothing else that really stated pre-amnesia Frank Todd was that much of a Stu Homemaker. The living room section (which the stairs led into directly) held a T.V. with a few video game systems, couches and a bean bag. The bedroom portion was incredibly lavish, a humongous bed set against the wall, facing out towards the largest of the windows and towards the sunrise. A workout "room" had been established along the windows, with various bits of free weights and esoteric exercise paraphernalia lining the floor, and the windows themselves were immaculately clean, covered over by a series of the same kind of black, silk-looking material that covered the bed itself. A bit of a ways off what I could consider to be the 'bedroom' nearest the kitchen was a large net-like hammock that had been strung from one wall across the room to the ceiling: either it was for sleeping or climbing, I hadn't a clue.

Here and there along the walls were bookshelves packed full of books, some that struck me as being...a bit odd. As I walked towards the center of the living space, it dawned on me that this didn't cover the entire second floor, for all that it felt like it; the open-air plan really threw my senses off. It was almost as if I HAD been able to somehow alter my perception though, I could see the rest of it, whatever I was using the second floor for. My silent musings then broke harshly as I realized I wasn't alone between one moment and the next. Whirling into a crouch, my fingers flexing, I prepared to throw myself into a fight only to draw myself short, my breath catching.

The beautiful, ebony-skinned woman gazed about the room slowly, as if not seeing me at all, nor at the shock of recognition plastered on my stupid face. Stupid was certainly the word for it – stupid I felt, and wool-headed, and all at once a series of incredibly personal and intimate memories flooded me and my Voice, damn near overpowering me as much as her presence had.

Taboo 0: Cliché of Memories

The woman wasn't that tall, perhaps five-foot-five, but her shoulders spoke of a quiet strength and her aura was gigantic, her presence breathtaking. Her hands and ankles were slim, I knew that, and her back and buttocks were strong - her hips were somewhat wide, having aided her in giving birth multiple times even as she could use them for stability in a killing blow. What little makeup she wore was either nonexistent or so classy that I couldn't tell - those lips of hers, though, they stood out full and a dark raspberry color. Her breasts were shapely and sweet, and her breath - my head swam with the flavor of strawberries and cherries, cheerfully shared with artistic passion.

Passion. I could feel my libido kick into overdrive and, for once, I was glad that my Voice hadn't chosen now to try and butt in with a stupid joke or comment.

Her neck was strong yet slim, her limbs graceful yet full, and her face...my god, how many poems had I written about her beauty? The fullness of her lips, the sweet shape of her face, the soft chocolate brown color of her eyes that...that...

"Wait, didn't her eyes change color or somethin' like that?" My Voice asked me breathlessly, even as her eyes did indeed darken in a whirl of black. I frowned, wondering at how he...it...I?...could know that. Her eyes were definitely dark now, and they moved about the room with a strange, patient power, a knowledge that I somehow

The Generalist

lacked.

For whatever reason I found that slightly galling and, hanging onto that emotion, was able to find my angry side again. Puffing myself up to prepare for a verbal attack, full of questions, like why this woman was in my house, she instead cut me off with a strangely familiar manner, her speaking patterns even and without betraying a hint of emotion beyond that thinly-veiled sense of hidden knowledge.

"Thomas, why aren't you answering your phone?" Though her eyes were busy taking in the room in that slow, devouring manner, I somehow knew she was talking to me despite the name that clearly wasn't mine. I was Frank Todd, wasn't I? I zoned back in as she continued, "I've tried calling you all day. Daniel said he hasn't seen you since yesterday evening, and Abbacus has foreseen great danger to you. The bones warned me to come here," her eyes finally settled on me with a strange weight, as if her very gaze had a gravity all of its own, "and I'm starting to understand why."

After pulling my own gaze away from those raspberry-red lips of hers, I realized that she was wearing clothes - it was only those weird memories that made me think she was nude. Black leather pants, a long purple sleeveless shift with gold lace (no buttons, only those laces - some strange kinda old style?) that ended in a hoodie which she

Taboo 0: Cliché of Memories

currently had up over what I knew would be dark, long cornrows. I could see the iron buckles at the tops of her collared boots, and tight gloves of black leather - the shift itself was barely a scrap of cloth, revealing interesting peeks at her well-shaped sides. A wide, black leather belt at her waist brought the long shift in tight against her luscious curves.

"Your aura is full of holes, Thomas."

I blinked, the desirable scent of her clogging my nose. I shook my head slightly and patted the back of it with the heel of my palm - something was up, and even as everything about me screamed to feel her in my arms, her lips against mine, the taste of her in my mouth, something equally as primal was telling me that she was as dangerous as they come.

A brotha could seriously fall for someone like her, and I was getting the sinking suspicion that brotha was me.

"Thomas, what's wrong? You haven't reacted like this since...well," she wet her lips with the tip of her tongue, an unconscious act, as she gazed back at me with slight confusion in her sweet eyes. My god, the look did adorable things for her, "Ever. Why is your aura so full of holes?"

I took a deep breath, centering myself in more ways than one and began my tirade, "Look, lady...I don't know

The Generalist

who this Thomas guy is, but I think you've got me mistaken for someone else. Lucky bastard, whoever he is. I don't know who any of these people you're speakin' of are, but I'm certain that there's someone out there who can help you - I'm, sadly, not the guy for ya. Sorry. And my aura, or whatever, feels absolutely fine thanks - I'm just not who you think I am."

As I spoke, her eyes betrayed nothing until I mentioned that I wasn't the guy for her. For a moment quite a bit of hurt flashed through those dark eyes of hers before returning to their normal mode of grave consideration - it dawned on me suddenly that I really, REALLY wanted to be Thomas, if anything just to see that she didn't feel that kinda hurt again.

She frowned and suddenly the considering look turned into a disapproving one, and I bit back the urge to gulp as she growled in that velvety voice of hers, "Thomas, this isn't funny. Daniel is worried sick about you and besides - you left your gloves at the Hold. I came by to drop them off and find out what's going on myself only to find you gazing about the Shop as if you've never been here before!"

When did she draw so close to me? When did I think it was okay to let this strange woman get close to me the way she did, her legs moving her luscious form about as if on coiled springs?

Taboo 0: Cliché of Memories

Her arms came up around my neck and my body relaxed; she drew me down to her and kissed me deep, my eyes closing naturally even as she melted into my arms. Time stopped, completely and utterly, and I knew what was wrong.

The kiss flared through me, liquid lightning in my veins, and I felt both hot and cold as it dawned on me that her kiss was for both myself and my Voice. With that realization came many, many more, and the connection that lay between us tore through my mind, showing me the man that I was, grinning back at me with that vicious, rat bastard grin of his. Mine. Whatever.

Her eyes suddenly flew open at the heated exchange that occurred during the kiss and I immediately flung myself out the window in an empowered jump, time standing still as I moved in the space between seconds in my fear, desperate to get away from her and the memories that kiss slammed back into my itching brain. I heard her cry out my name, this time my real name, as I crossed my arms over my head and felt the glass shatter and give way, my hand flicking out to grasp and scrabble at the wall for purchase before kicking away from it, intent on getting away from her.

Getting away from The Priestess before any more of those blasted memories obliterated my mind, my soul!

The Generalist
****

"Okay, that was a bit dramatic," I thought to myself.

"Monsters, FBI files, beautiful priestesses throwing themselves at us. We're a pair of real jokers, we are! Real aces," my Voice replied to me as I settled myself into a diner some miles away from The Shop. I had entered one, only to be hailed by name by an incredibly cute, pale blonde waitress. At this point in time I hadn't wanted to be noticed any more until I worked my way through everything I gained from The Priestess during that kiss. Waving at the waitress and greeting her with a chuckle and a smile, I slipped out the back and headed out for a few miles, intent on simply getting away from the nearby grid of people who apparently knew me on sight.

The kiss. Everything between us started with that kiss years ago, and to this day she still had a hold over me. A priestess in name and position, as well as the avatar of three different goddesses. When she kissed me it had brought everything rushing back to me, as far as what memories I had of her, her husband, and the religious organization they fronted.

Not all those memories were pleasant, and that's what had frightened me. At the time I thought she was the

Taboo 0: Cliché of Memories

source of those monstrosities, the terrors I had once faced, for indeed face them down I did - I saw it through her own eyes, having witnessed this very form of mine pitting itself physically, mentally and spiritually against monstrosities like the creature I ran from in the alleyway.

My God, was that who I was? Was that Frank Todd? Some kinda monster hunter, as well as everything else?!

"It might be who you are."

By now I was kinda done with surprises. In the very least, I wasn't shocked at the old, gray-haired portly guy that now sat across from me at my diner table. I looked about and saw no one else nearby outside of ourselves except for the bored waitress. I had chosen the diner because of how standard it looked (a counter with the kitchen right behind it, bar stools, tables with those weird conjoined chairs lining the walls and a few standalone tables and chairs in the middle, and mostly bored customers picking at their food, drinking coffee, and just getting through the long night) in the hopes that I could be left alone to figure out this recent rush of information.

And then God sat across from me, popping in out of thin air, leafing through a menu and murmuring aloud about how pricey this place was.

"I mean, I know you've got your cash and I have mine, but at these prices? And the drinks aren't even free? Pah,"

The Generalist

God made a rude noise, but waved over the waitress who came over and looked only at me, gnawing on her bubble gum.

"Is the steak and eggs not to your liking, mister?" she asked me. I had already devoured the food and was simply nursing the somewhat palatable coffee. Nursing as in holding the mug and staring into the delicious-smelling liquid, gathering my thoughts quietly.

God nodded to her knowingly, "Yes, the steak and eggs are excellent, Marjorie. I'd like to have a plate of that myself. Is the bacon and sausage here kosher?"

Marjorie (she wasn't wearing a nametag, a tired redhead in a pinstripe blouse and skirt, real old school diner gear) replied to me, her tired brown eyes beginning to look at me suspiciously, "What does that mean? No, it's local. Good stuff too."

God chuckled at the bad joke and handed her the menu, which she took without looking at It at all, "Good, good! Oy, I'd like a double of that and a swig of brandy in the coffee would be nice, darlin'. *Vaya con Dios*, eh?"

She frowned at me and took off, leaving me to eyeball God a bit more. It was dressed horribly with Its semi-portly, short frame stuffed into a Hawaiian shirt, gray trousers, flip-flops and a business suit jacket over the shirt. God apparently preferred to be of graying, advanced years

Taboo 0: Cliché of Memories

yet still have a head full of hair - out of all Its looks, this one and the one of me were Its most-used appearances. It was clean-shaven, and Its' reddish skin held a strange sheen to it.

It also expected me to tip. I didn't know why I knew this, but the bastard never tipped - It'd pay full price for Its' meal, then expect me to tip. It also knew the trick of how to read minds, but never used it out of respect to others and the ideal of free will, even amongst those who didn't worship It.

"That's because it's impolite, my boy, it's impolite," God began to count out dollar bills from Its strangely large hands, the fingernails immaculate despite the calluses' on the fingers and palms, "I mean, how would I feel if you simply started picking through my brain and blasted yours to bits with what you found there? No, Franky boy, it's just not right."

I frowned, then remarked stupidly, "You're God."

"And you're quick. What is this, twenty questions? God Itself is before you, and all you can do is ask me if I'm God or not? Oy, what a pain in my *toucas* you are sometimes, Franky boy!"

I frowned harder, and my Voice asked, "*If you're God, can you help us out then? We can't remember much, well anything at all really, and things are just getting worse.*"

The Generalist

"But of course I can, my friend!" The voice that rang back in my head was a bit more like what I'd expected of a monotheistic deity, full of power and pomp. It also almost blew my head apart, but I somehow accepted God's mind-voice as easily as I did my own Voice, *"First and foremost though, let me ask you of what you've done in the past five hours since waking up. Perhaps in that story you will find the answer you seek, eh?"*

"Well, we figured out a bit more of our history. We've run from a monster. We've kissed a beautiful pagan princess and have jumped out of a second story window of our own place. But right now it feels like we've run into a wall - I haven't any real clue as to figure out what I've done in the past twenty-four hours to awaken in a place like what I did, why I can't remember anything truly significant, and am without any real leads towards that end."

"Well. Well, well, well," God smacked Its lips and tapped a strange beat on the orange tabletop. I realized that I hadn't actually looked into Its eyes, but when I did they were a cold, icy blue color. God gazed about the diner, Its eyes settling on this object and that, almost as if trying to remember what they were amidst a lexicon of other items before looking back at me, "Since my boys were the ones who did you, I shall tell you what you want to know! But I can only tell you so much, the Pact of the Pantheons and what-not. But, and I say it again, since my

Taboo 0: Cliché of Memories

boys did this to you, I'll tell you!"

I frowned at that, remembering the note of Catholic Church involvement on my FBI file. God, either not noticing or caring about the frown, exclaimed loudly when Marjorie the waitress showed up with Its plate full of steak, eggs, and deep fried hash browns with the side order of both crispy bacon and sausage. She winked at me and went back to the kitchen with a skip in her step, promising coffee. God, for all that It looked like the type to be a bit more elegant, dug into the food with gusto and I almost found myself sharing Its delight.

"Oh, OH! Yes, this is definitely one of the finer aspects of the Physical Realm, my boy! Though nothing beats manna, especially with agave nectar, but hey I'll never complain over properly prepared t-bones with some eggs! HAH! Delicious! And this sausage and bacon - a bit extra, but so worth it!" God continued the commentary as It ate, Its voice continuing on even as It filled Its face, a miracle in and of itself without the use of any truly divine power. With Its infectious smile, I figured that this was Its way of keeping me calm despite the show of eating while talking with Its mouth closed - not a ventriloquist trick. I should know, I remembered knowing that trick myself. Hell, it worked on my Voice at least, who listened to God with rapt, yet comfortable, attention. Marjorie returned and poured me a second cup as well as getting God's coffee, and as she walked away I noticed that she looked a lot less

The Generalist
tired and a lot more desirable than she had earlier.

"So, where was I? Oh yeah, my bullyboys. Not the Mormons, they're just weird - the Catholics. Yeah, you're right on the nose with that one Frank, but due to the nature of what's been done to you I can't tell you anything really, outside of that, Peters' Church is involved and wants what you got. I wish I could tell you why they want it, but the whole Pact of Pantheons gig, y'know? Even then it's not like they'd do what I say when I say it, they haven't done what I wanted since way back in the day, before that King James asshole screwed with everything. Y'know I really did write that book, right? 'Divinely inspired' my holy feet, the backbiting bastard got me good before copyrights were ever invented!" God slammed Its fist into the table, making it shudder and an earthquake occur elsewhere in the city.

I frowned and rubbed at my chin, then pulled out the flask that had been comfortably warming my back pocket since God showed up, "This. This is what they fucked my memory up for?"

God's big, brown eyes widened as It spotted the flask, recognition in Its gaze, "Yeah, that's the Artifact alright! A pretty big one too, huh. Haven't seen it in a good long time too! No wonder they want you dead or alive for this 'un. Anyway, put that away or it's the Vatican Warlock Assassins time, there's a good lad!"

Taboo 0: Cliché of Memories

Ignoring the whole Vatican warlock assassin thing (really? really, God? Charlie Sheen quotes? What's next, Chuck Norris facts?), I slipped the strange flask back into my back pocket, frowning at my coffee before responding, "So. This thing is connected to the church and my memory loss? Something they did or the artifact?"

"A little of both, my boy, a little of both!" God chuckled and dabbed at Its chin with a handkerchief, the black gloves on Its large hands strangely familiar as It stood up, taller than earlier and with far more muscle and padding, "Y'know, I really do need to go check my hair and see if Marjorie still likes negroids. If she doesn't, it's her loss - tonight's Friday night, after all! Gonna get laid, then ski-ball at my usual spot."

And so God left me in that diner all alone and headed in Marjorie's general direction, having left enough money to pay for Its dinner yet leaving me to pay for the tip, wearing my face to once again go chat up some down-on-her-luck slottie whose life would become better for Its involvement. After Its dalliance, It would change genders and go play Ski-Ball until it was excruciatingly late, then hang out with teenagers and young adults at some beach bonfire. Eventually God's vacation days, due once a month, would be up and It would head back to Heaven to bully angels and heathens about, growling about how long it's been since there's been a good smiting.

The Generalist

Great. I frowned at the cup of coffee, realizing I hadn't had a single sip since getting it. Where the hell had it gone?

Standing up and counting out some cash, I slipped out of the diner with my hands in my pockets, remembering how God had looked exactly like me except for one thing.

The gloves. THOSE gloves. My gloves.

Ignoring the giggling from within the diner (God really was a quick work!), I knew where I had to go to get them.

I saw it, and knew exactly where it was, from the memories I inherited from the Priestess's kiss, the failed attempt to connect on the psionic level between herself, myself, the Voice, and the three goddesses she represented.

I had to go to the Hold of the Asture and get my damned gloves back. Those gloves were the key, the secret to my memory loss, and instinctively I just knew I had to get them back.

****

Taboo 0: Cliché of Memories
Round 3

It didn't take me long to make my way back to The Shop and grumble about the damage I did to my own window. These reflexes of mine were going to get me killed, and apparently it HAD at several points during the missions I had run with the Priestess. Yay for past memories.

Entering into the building again, I stopped silent and still as I realized several things. Firstly, the Priestess had indeed left with the gloves, just as I had thought she would, feeling more comfortable and secure keeping one of my greatest weapons in a place she felt strongest. Secondly, I hadn't needed the cold iron key this time (where the hell did I put that thing?) and my defenses didn't check me.

Thirdly, the monster from the alleyway earlier was sitting behind the secretary's desk, the phone made miniscule in its incredibly oversized hand as it spoke into a bluetooth headset.

"Wait, what? No, he just showed up - boss, don't freakin' run, okay? Just a minute. What? No, not you. Look, I'll talk to you later, okay?"

The creature set the phone down and stood up slowly, its hands kept where I could see them, "Okay...I know

The Generalist

things look weird, boss, but really, honestly I didn't know you'd react that way! If I had known you wanted to be THAT solo on this job, I'd've not tailed ya. Guess I still can't shake you properly yet, right?"

I frowned, ascertaining several implications from the creatures' dialogue. I spoke slowly, wanting to know one last thing before I simply ran on assumptions, "Why...did you roar my name like that earlier?"

The trollish humanoid blushed slightly, the red standing out against its dark green flesh as it rubbed the back of its head, spiky greenish hair slipping between its fingers, "Aw, bro...you oughta know I hate cardio. Makes me cranky, and I was kind of pissed that you were able to spot me so quick. Guess I'm still learning how to control these troll-motions and stuff, y'know? HUH!" the creature began to pelvis-thrust to the side, almost making me bolt again if not for the sheer absurdity of the situation.

"...okay. I'm going to level with you," I frowned and sat down on one of the chairs closest to the door, ready to make my move and run the hell out of there if the troll insomuch as batted an eye wrong, "I don't know who you are, I don't know who I am, and today has been one sincerely fucked up day."

The creature frowned, then noticed my hands for the first time as I rubbed them together for warmth, "Hey,

Taboo 0: Cliché of Memories

boss...where's your gloves and why aren't you wearing them? You never NOT wear them," he frowned and looked back at my eyes, "You ain't a changeling again, are you? I thought we killed all of ya from that clutch that hatched last month."

I groaned, holding my head with both palms, "What? No, what the...no, just no. No, I'm me. I've just had to relearn who I am, relent that I am what I am, and apparently I need to get this thing I woke up with to the Catholics in order to get my memory back. I don't remember you, I don't remember that priestess hottie earlier, but I know I need my gloves back and she's got 'em at this Hold of hers. I figured to come back here and search one of the 'puters for the Hold's location, since I can't seem to remember-"

"Oh, that's pro'lly the magics and what-not, boss. Not even you can figure out how they can do it, but it's that kind of sympathetic magic which helps them - a mystical version of your very own 'Not Here, Not Me' trick," the troll sat down again and began to type at a keyboard made of laser light on the desk - despite the sheer power of those massive armored fingers and the sharpness of his claws, he seemed to be incredibly adept at speed-typing and in no time at all had called up the information I needed, doing no damage at all to the desk.

Which I was suddenly thankful for because now that I

The Generalist

had a chance to look at it closer, I noticed that the thing was freakin' mahogany, and expensive at that, all full of subtle intricate detail-work to boot!

"Alright boss! She left the usual dead drop info, and I got the address where the Hold is currently. Since it's Catholics we shouldn't worry about gettin' kitted out or anything, but perhaps if you got Holy Diver or Benediction just in case-"

"Wait, what?" I frowned at the troll, realizing that both I and my Voice had somehow already become accustomed to his strange presence, as if he'd always been here for us, "Look, dude, I dunno-"

"Dash."

I blinked, "What?"

"Dash. My name's Dash. Daniel 'Dash' Hopkins - I used to be the fastest motherfucker you knew, for all that I hated cardio," he chuckled and held out that humongous hand towards me, "We've been friends for, Jesus, damn near a decade. For what it's worth, sorry 'bout earlier bro - like I said, the whole troll thing got me, and I didn't realize you weren't...uh, you. Guess it's what bein' friends are about, right? Fuckin' up and still bein' cool."

I frowned and considered that with his reach and my inability to fight back against such a monstrous strength,

Taboo 0: Cliché of Memories

this troll, Dash, could've probably killed me ever since I came back to the Shop. I took a gamble and shook his hand - though his hand was different than I remember it being, he was right. We HAD been friends for years, it only took until now for me to remember that vital fact.

    I hooked my thumb with his, changing the handshake into a new grip before sliding back and bumping fists with him, ending it with a snap of the fingers. The Handshake done, he nodded as if the past some-odd hours hadn't happened, "So. Holy Diver, Benediction...your usual stuff won't work against humans, but the ol' Fist to Face always does the trick! And if it's the church, there's bound to be Vatican Warlock Assassins too! 'S gonna be fun, boss!"

    I frowned, "What are you talking about, and not you too! Look, the Charlie Sheen quotes weren't funny when God said 'em, and now-"

    "Oh, OH no! Yeah, Catholics," Dash frowned, "If God bothered to warn you, then we should possibly bring Ash instead of Holy Diver. They're always a good combo against Catholics. Plus Vee hates Holy Diver anywhere near her Hold and Abba digs Ash."

    I'm fairly certain the look of absolute stupid on my face is what stopped him and urged him to explain to me what he was talking about. Artificing (of which I was apparently an Artificer, a person who can make these

The Generalist

things) was the art of creating artifacts using prayer or spiritual energies, ki energy, psionic energy, magic, or any combination of the four. Evidently I was one of the few people on the planet who could use all four in order to create artifacts of noteworthy strength, usable by just about anyone who picked them up and knew how to activate them.

Amongst them were my Holy Diver, a pair of silver knuckles that bears a specialized script engraved during the smelting process itself. Instead of normal water, holy water was used during the creation of the knuckles, giving them even further divinely destructive capability against the ethereal. It also radiated with Gods' wrath, usually upsetting gods and avatars of other pantheons.

Benediction, made from the melted silver cross used to kill Vlad Tepes himself, is a six-shooter useful against just about anything and everything paranormal, shaped to resemble a .357 Smith and Wesson Magnum. The fact that the gun itself also housed other secrets and bore eldritch script on the pommel also annoyed me, since I hadn't a clue what the secrets were, nor how to access them, nor what the script said. Dash calmed me down though, apparently used to my flash anger issues - when I regained my memories, I'd learn how to access Benedictions' secrets once more, or so he told me.

Apparently the gun had been made by mixing my own

Taboo 0: Cliché of Memories

blood into its creation, the revolver's black grip as much a puzzle as it was a weapon, created by a brilliant, yet mad, designer who owed me way back in the day.

And Ash, a whitewood staff of unknown power and ability. The staff itself housed the spirit of Shiro, a 'white dog spirit' I had bound to the thing, a poor soul unable to pass over to wherever she was supposed to go after this life. For whatever reason, I apparently thought it'd be better off being useful as a helper to me then languishing about wherever it was she was originally anchored.

"The only problem is that I haven't a clue how to access your Artifacts Room, or at least I don't off-the-top-of-my-head remember," Dash frowned at me while continuing to make sandwiches in our shared kitchen. One of the things he had pointed out to me was that outside of being something of a bodyguard and valet to me, he was also something of a sous chef, proud of his skill at cooking and willing to pound anyone who said otherwise, "I'm not the Esper, you are. Only Espers can access it, 'pparently."

I frowned from where I was sitting at the island counter, noting how he was haphazardly piling meats and cheeses on top of tomatoes and pickles, "What does that have to do with anything? And...can I ask you what happened to you, Dash? Why you look like...well...," I coughed nervously at the weak ending.

The Generalist

Dash chuckled and waved a butter knife covered in deli mustard, "You'll probably remember this later on, so I'll give you the quick breakdown of things. You ready bro? Alright, here:

Nigh on five years ago, there's no warning or anythin', just suddenly everything happens at once. Monster-genes, people who are the descendants of monsters and other beings from thousands of centuries back, are suddenly activating and undergoing Metamorphosis all over the place. Ghosts and goblins and all sortsa other things are causin' chaos, and all sorts of Old World Beings are suddenly making their move, right? The Havoc of 2012, fun for everyone.

The guv'ment, so to speak, gets smart and releases the Black File, a dossier packed to the gills proving that they've known about Fae, magic, psionics, ki energy and more ever since, hell...the twenties. It also bears a shitton of contracts passed onto them by the old Templar Ordeli...uh, the Knights Templar...and the Rosicrucian's. Y'know, the Order of the Rosy Cross, the guys who trained you in the Army in mysticism and stuff?

What, you don't remember...OH YEAH, memory loss," the troll groaned against a huge palm before turning back to his work, washing his hands again before working at a second sandwich for himself. Though my mouth was full of delicious sandwich, apparently he still saw the stupid

Taboo 0: Cliché of Memories

radiating from my face at the whole mysticism part, "Anyway, the government makes a call out for every hunter, slayer, and whatever-have-you to band together to present a united human front. The best part is when it's revealed that various organizations are rumored to be behind the sudden outbreak of Monster-gene activation and interdimensional bullshittery, chiefest amongst them being the once-secret Department XIII of the Catholic Church, 'Iscariot,' the guys who usually lead exorcisms and artifact hunts.

Despite that little scandal they worked out a deal where the government would allow them to continue the artifact hunts and have certain other freedoms in their pursuit of their own clandestine ends, all the while providing services to the hunters, slayers, pagans and more. This was mostly at the urging of the United Theist Council, an actually somewhat peaceful council of, like, every religion in the world or some shit.

Anyway, lots of stuff happened and today you have licensed exorcists, artifact hunters, monster slayers, and more. Mostly they follow one of the four basic food groups of ki energy, psionics, magic, or spiritual faith but all are pretty much universal in one thing: that humanity deserves the place we've carved out for ourselves here on this planet, and all these Old World fucktards are going to have to accept the current dynasty under heaven instead of trying to pound us back into the Dark Ages, or the Grimm

The Generalist

Times some of us call it. Five guesses as to why, buddy."

Dash chuckled and sat down heavily on the bean bag, devouring his own sandwich as I followed close, listening with rapt attention and hopefully not showing how ignorant I was of all this mess, "Naturally people still ignore what's right in front of 'em, yah? Hell, I didn't even know I was a Monster-gene, or that any of this shit existed, 'til one damn near took my head off - then I activated, and my body underwent Metamorphosis but my mind stayed human, see? You helped me out big time on that one, Frank, and I haven't fully thanked you for it too. You couldn't turn me back to being human, but at least I get to keep my mind, and for that I'm grateful."

I frowned but accepted it. Hell, all this other crazy shit was pretty...well, crazy, so what's one more absurd thing?

"What about the Asture?" I asked, finishing off my sandwich and heading over to make another. I frowned, realizing that I was STILL hungry as fuck!

"What, the tree-huggers? Norse religion, worshipers of Odin and Thor and stuff. Rollin' bones, makin' runes, castin' magic. Each Hold is important to them because you can't have a proper Hold without having a live clipping of Yggdrasil, the World Tree, and it takes a lot to keep 'em alive away from Yggdrasil. It's why the title of Runesmith is so important, since they're the guys who do that part. It

Taboo 0: Cliché of Memories

gives them tons of power, but they rarely travel away from their Holds - the entire Asture are an awful lot like Fae or elves in that the further away from their source, the weaker they get. Even Vee...uh, Vorel...'the Priestess' you called her earlier...can get uncomfortable if she's not near another Hold.

Anyway, you probably saw that yourself though, right? Seein' yourself through Vee's eyes and all that."

I frowned, thinking back. There were still plenty of angles I didn't quite understand, like how the Priestess - er, Vorel - could be with me the way she was and yet be happily married to Abbacus Keith, the Runesmith of the Los Angeles Hold. I finished making the sandwich and remembered how she looked, how she smelled just standing there earlier.

Like cherries, like strawberries.

"Of fire, dark flesh and relentless motion, undulating and awash in waves of pure delightful passion..."

I mentally punched my Voice and asked Dash, "So. After the grub, we're heading over there to get my gloves? What's so special about 'em?"

"Woah, woah-HO! I don't even know where to begin with 'em, bro," Dash chewed thoughtfully, "First off, you punch ghosts with it. Like, for all that you swear up and

The Generalist

down that your 'arts' are so artsy and aesthetic and artistic, in the end you do what I do to most people and just punch face with it. Seriously. I've seen you do a ton of stuff with 'em though, and you list them off as your greatest Artifacts to date. I know this for a fact - as a troll, most energy types can seriously fuck my day up but I can see in the magic realm as good as any magus, and as a martial artist I learned how to manipulate ki energy. Great for the reiki, little use for anything else though," he chuckled at that, then continued, "From what I've seen, you've done something incredibly strange to them with your own ki. I can't tell what else beyond that though."

He frowned at me then, an incredibly frightening thing if I wasn't already so used to his mannerisms, "Bro...why haven't you entered Psycho Space and opened up the Armory? We gotta git."

I frowned back at him, my glower a comfortable thing to my face (was I always this mean and curmudgeonly?) before his broke and he groaned, slapping his forehead into both palms, "Memory...loss. Shit. You don't know how to...OH CRAP!" Sudden realization hit him, "You don't know how to USE your stuff! Your abilities! Hell, even the Artifacts!"

I frowned harder and merely nodded my head, suddenly feeling very small and afraid despite my bulk. He reached over and clasped my shoulder, making me feel smaller as

Taboo 0: Cliché of Memories

he considered, "...I know you left Benediction in the car, but all the bullets we usually use are in the Armory. Silver casings, bullets of blessed stained glass, oil, rosemary, thyme, silver shavings, garlic - just about every trope and stereotype packed into a single bullet," he murmured aloud, rubbing at his all-too-human jaw, the scales glinting, "But I should have some backup training ammo in the trunk. When shot out of Benny, they're still gonna hit targets like cannonballs, even if you can't activate the gun as an artifact properly. I've got Big Boy - uh, my baseball bat artifact - in the trunk as well. Until we get your gloves, we really shouldn't try to access the Armory, certainly not until you get your memory back, bro!"

Following the troll down the stairs I suddenly paused for a moment at the top, something frightening hitting me with the force of a hammer to the face, "...Dash?"

He stopped and blinked up at me, and I noticed for the first time that despite the alien, armored scales and green skin that he really was a handsome kinda guy, the scales on his cheeks and chin accentuating the more human parts of his face, "Yeah? 'Sup?"

"...dude. I - will I be...me? I mean, am I...me?"

"Can anyone truly be themselves?" my Voice responded to me.

"Dude, you seem to be you. I mean, your personality,

The Generalist

right? Yeah. You're you and you're always you," Dash offered a dazzlingly bright grin, "It's like you always say, no matter what, you're you. Frank Todd, right? C'mon bro, let's go."

I took that to heart, not only that this was the kind of man that I was and apparently still am, but that those who considered me friend could depend on that so much, could trust that I'd always be me. Strangely enough, in the consistency this implied to me there lay a great comfort, something I hadn't felt since I woke up in that bathtub full of blood.

****

"Oh, oh shit. Oh SHIT! You are going to fucking LOVE this!" Ever since we had entered into the "garage," an underground feature that emptied out into another street several blocks away, Dash had been all scary, jagged-toothed smiles, "It's almost like Christmas all over again! I mean, well, you're usually not one for money - usually I'm the guy who handles that portion, if at all. Unless it's loan-sharking, you like that. And the knee-capping. But yeah, you're usually not one for material wealth but ohhhhh boy. This one you were adamant about."

Something only vaguely car-shaped but pointier in

Taboo 0: Cliché of Memories

places lay under a tarp in the middle of this expansive garage space. The walls were lined with tools, and the place had the feel of a rich mechanic's wet dream - powered lifts on the floor, power tools of all shapes and sizes everywhere, bright overhead lighting with portable bright lights, and an air system. The floor and walls looked like some kind of strange concrete, which struck me as a strange thing. If you could afford all this wonder, why go with a material like that? Despite the concrete, it looked like someone had taken a mechanic shop and just air-lifted the damn thing into this basement area.

"Uh, this whole place?" I waved a hand about, generally indicating the garage.

"What? No. No, this. Our baby," Dash chuckled and gently stroked whatever lay under the tarp, leaning over to kiss what I could only approximate was the hood, "Dude, the third member of our team. The awesomest of awesomeness, the most excellent of excellence. The most illegally operating vehicle in all of Los Angeles, bruddah!"

I frowned, but I'm fairly certain the excitement building up within me was more from Dash's enthusiasm than any memory I'd regained by now. At least, I think it was!

And then he unveiled her, slowly at first but then with a flourish.

Her.

The Generalist

The Roadbuster.

The tarp was pure silk. Now I knew why.

I realized I was breathless, and I'm fairly certain I wasn't a car guy...but hell, anyone would be!

This wasn't a car. The lines were as gently curved as a beautiful woman, working back from the double grill-piece (which looked bigger than I remember) along the stylized hood, as well-made as any car I've ever seen. But this wasn't a car, this simply was NOT a simple car! How does one describe a rose to a blind person?

It had four wheels, obviously high-priced and a custom job of some sort. It had a strange make to the body itself, one that emphasized clean lines, hell it even had a fin in the back. The lights in the front and the array of lights in the back spoke of high power, and while the grill screamed one kind of car, the headlights spoke of another, a custom body job. As I drew closer to the vehicle, I noticed a strange thing with the paint job - depending on where I looked, her color was either a pitch black coloration or dark cherry red!

"Pricey," my Voice said. I, for the life of me, was simply struck dumb by the beauty of the car itself.

Dash's voice was reverent, a petitioner worshiping at the altar of his goddess, "She's based on the 2012 model,

Taboo 0: Cliché of Memories

before the chaos. She's a Ford Mustang, the Shelby GT 500 Super Snake, one of the last Mustangs in this century before Ford got bought out by those foreign leeches."

"Vampires?"

"Politicians. But her, HER! Her name is The Roadbuster. Practically everything about her is a custom job. A V-12 Cummings Engine. We've got her maxed out at 850 horses. The paint job on her is the two-tone type, changes from pitch black to red depending on what angle you're lookin' at her from. A tungsten-carbide roll cage and chassis, with a carbon-fiber shell. 6-speed variable transmission. That beautiful red interior you're ogling is all aniline leather, no vinyl whatsoever, with racer seatbelts. The steering wheel is detachable, 'cuz of the custom-made one you got for my hands. The body kit is my own recipe, imported Ford and Aston Martin kit pieces from Detroit and London. Did I mention the panty-smashing sound system? Yeah. Panty. Smashing.

Bro, we've faced down some pretty nasty things. You wanted a car that was both lightweight enough for me to pick up and use as a weapon, but heavy enough for you to hit me in my full berserker rage with enough force and power to snap me out of it, and fast enough to keep up with whatever we're chasing down. We've got both nitrous oxide and a turbo-charger in her. We've got a James Bond assortment of weapon drops in the back: sharpened

The Generalist

caltrops, oil slick, smoke screen, holy water, silver shavings that double as chaff and electronic counter measures, as well as more than a couple of nastier drops," he began to walk around the car, stroking her lovingly as he spoke. Indeed as I followed around I realized once again that the paint really did change from a pitch black to a dark cherry red as I moved! This wasn't a Mustang, she was a freakin' monster!

He continued on, ignoring me completely, his eyes all for her - as were my own, "Also, she comes with your hand-crafted divine glyphs, stuff from your mystic training, y'know? Like in the Long Hallway back at The Shop. Those rows of shelving that were bought by yours truly? Modified and tweaked by you. You have divine glyphs printed all over the clear coat AND on the roll cage itself, all of 'em having saved our lives more than once in the recent past, bro.

We've got variable weaponry of all sorts we can put on her, but usually we're all the weaponry we need. You've gone out of your way to ensure that The Roadbuster is one sweet, lean, mean, fighting machine and as one of her head mechanics, I've done my damndest to ensure she stays sweet."

As I drew closer to the car, I began to feel the now-familiar sensation of strange things a-doin' at the peripherals of my vision, my brain becoming itchy as red

Taboo 0: Cliché of Memories

glyphs began to appear over the paint job and along what I could see of the roll cage. For a moment it felt as if the itchiness would turn into a hard burn, then abruptly faded, as did the glowing glyphs that were previously floating on the car. Dash chuckled and I drew back from the car slightly, nervous after what just happened.

Dash grinned at the car, "Oh, all that goodness and the Whammy Bar."

"Wait, a whammy bar? In the car?" I meant to blink stupidly at him, like I have been whenever I haven't a clue what's going on. Instead I merely stared at The Roadbuster, transfixed by beauty for the second time in so many hours.

"No. That," he pointed to the front and I realized what was so weird about the car, even though I had been staring at it the entire time. The Roadbuster had a battering-ram like grill, like the police cruisers used! "Remember what I said about me in my berserker state? That usually does it, right there. It's also good for all sortsa other stuff, and the whole thing is packed to the gills with secret prizes and such. We've GOT all the permits for everything, and also both of us have C.C.W's – conceal/carry. Uh, licenses to carry hidden weapons. The car's also got C.C.W.'s as well."

"She's got C.C.W.'s?" I finally tore my gaze away from

The Generalist

her to look at him incredulously.

"Yeah," he chuckled and patted her side affectionately, "Rhonda F. Buster-Hopkins, F for 'Fuckin' A,' not 'Ford.' You might be her daddy, but I'm her poppa, y'dig? You're as mechanically inclined with her as you are with a toaster, and every time you try to fix the toaster you turn it into an interdimensional hell-gate for the Shoggoths. No, bro, you're a great driver but you're absolutely shit when it comes to repair, ergo why I got to claim her."

"...Rhonda?" I lifted an eyebrow, "Why don't we just call her 'Rhonda?'"

"Because 'Rhonda' is kinda close to 'Road,' and it's just her *nom de guerre* anyway, bro. This is The Roadbuster. Ya gotta say the whole thing, y'know?"

He opened the passenger-side door for me and grinned with what I was beginning to understand was a maniacal grin.

"Get in~!"

****

Let me tell you about Asture pagans, elves, and Fae. They're all three vicious, old, powerful, and extremely

Taboo 0: Cliché of Memories

proud. They're also all three bound to the land in some way or method, and the Asture were no strangers to having to move about on the fly, ever at the whims of land and the gods they worshiped. A Hold could be any place, an apartment or a park or a zoo, so long as the cutting of Yggdrasil had a place to settle momentarily.

It's also the place where those of the Asture faith gather to perform the various ceremonies, network, learn new skills and teach old ones, as well as to keep up the oral traditions of the heraldic skalds of yesteryear, recounting eddas (the oral stories and histories) of their people.

There were also many other services provided by the leaders, including direct communication to their gods, for all that the communication was mostly in tongues and had to be translated.

"The Reassignment of Babel," Dash nodded as he steered his way through late night L.A. traffic, "When the various Pantheons all tried to assert themselves all at the same goddamned time, alongside the monotheistic God, as the sole power of the world, they quickly came to the conclusion that if they continued to ignore each other they were going to incite the entire world into a destructive war. Suffice it to say, this would also screw over the prayers and worship they needed as they each came about the idea that such a thing as a world-wide series of crusades would only end in their own doom.

The Generalist

Instead, the Pact of the Pantheons came about, a truce that exists to ensure that all humanity, and more, gain the ability and freedom to serve and worship whomever they wish. A part of that is the Reassignment of Babel, which reinforces the need for Oracles and Translators alike - doesn't matter what you call 'em, so long as they're both involved. This limits how gods and such communicate with humanity in general, and only those truly willing to go through the process will stick around and be true to the faith. Don't confuse this with Avatars and such – all they do is give the pantheons a nice ticket to ride around on the Physical Plane. In order to do some serious hoodoo, they need to be in full-blown God mode, y'dig?"

I nodded in the passenger seat, taking all this in. I took a few moments of thought, chewing over the information while music drifted from the radio before speaking up, "But what about God, earlier? How did I get so comfortable with him?"

"Big G? You and It got somethin' special," Dash chuckled at me, his green eyes flicking this way and that, "Hell, you and half the spirit world and magic realms got some kind of special thing goin' on at one point in time or another. You cultivate contracts and negotiations the way some people cultivate prize petunias, bro. Don't even ask about Psycho Space, you're one of the biggest fish in this part of Los Angeles. Heh."

Taboo 0: Cliché of Memories

I frowned at that and noted, once again, that strange term, "Dude, what's...what the hell's a Psycho Space? You said that earlier."

"Man, memory loss is a bitch! Alright, here's the quick version since we're almost to the Hold: y'know that there's a Spirit World and a Magical Realm, right? Dimensions that exist alongside our current one, the Physical Plane, or Material Plane. Well, there's also one for psychics, like a mental Internet or somethin'. It's called the Psychic Realm, but you've always called it the Psycho Space, something about your sense of humor and how there's so many psychos cluttering the place up. You've told me before how it looks, but I've never been there m'self...somethin' about darkness and stars and shit. All I know 'bout it is that it exists, that everyone's mind is in it, and that only Espers can really do shit with it directly, like really high-level shit. You've noted before, though, that all four realms are affected by one another's resultant energy, like doing magic in the Psycho Space or prayers fucking with the Magic realm, and all four affecting the Material Plane. It's one of the reasons why you were called The Heretic for a bit of time. Heh, you've still got those newspaper clippings saved in your personal office."

"Office? I have an office back at The Shop?"

"Dude, what DON'T we got there?! The Shop is home - ain't no place like it!" The troll laughed, weaving about

The Generalist

professionally through traffic, and I then noticed how the steering wheel looked normal in his humongous hands, obviously a custom job, "I swear, comin' to work is, like, always the best bizness, y'know? I got my own place, but we crash and chillax at The Shop whenever there's nothin' on the docket. Rarely happens though since things are usually hoppin' and we've got bizness to handle on a weekly, if not daily, basis."

A part of me felt nettled by something at random, and it dawned on me that my Voice was replaying a memory from earlier. Focusing on it for a moment, I turned to Dash and asked, "Say, bro? Who's Thomas and why did that priestess woman call me him? I mean at the time I thought it was...well, uh-" I shut up, still not of a mind yet as to what that situation was about.

Dash looked aside at me and gave a dirty chuckle, "Heh-HAH! That'd be Vee, er...Vorel. Yeah, that's her pet name for you. Somethin' about the stuff you wrote under that name back in the day. She really dug it somethin' fierce."

"So, Dash...what are you to me?" I frowned, wanting to change the subject as carnal thoughts of the Priestess strangled me, unbidden, "I mean...you, like, some kinda super-butler?"

"BUTLER? Nigga, do I look like I buttle? I'm yer

Taboo 0: Cliché of Memories

friend, bro, and yer partner. We both handle different aspects of The Shop and all the services we render to our happy customers, y'dig? Yer good at a ton of shit, but you ain't the master of any of 'em, 'cept for a couple yer really good at. Yer great at martial arts, but hey - I'm better. But since I'm a troll, I'm usually the guy who handles the crowd control and the street sweepin'. Gimme a goon, and I'll bust 'em all up, y'know what I mean? But, because I'm a troll that means I'm really, REALLY, weak against energy-based attacks, y'know? Magic, spiritual attacks, ki energy (which sucks 'cuz I'm so good at ki m'self), psionics, they can all really fuck me up in a one-on-one battle. But physical? Bah, I've taken bullets to the skull and all it did was piss me off after I grew it back. My head, I mean.

I'm the driver, mostly the chef, kinda sorta bodyguard when we gotta act that shit out, a fellow knee-capper alongside yah, sparring partner, secretary - you HATE answering phones, and every time you get on the phone you get a little...uh, cranky. Scare off the customers. Mostly though, we're an equal partnership, 's why I handle the phones and you make the Artifacts, like my Big Boy in the trunk," he chuckled viciously at the mention of the baseball bat, "Reinforced silver, custom-ordered humongous for my hands, nasty little bitch with some kinetic skill on it or somethin'. Doubles the damage at point of impact, and can affect the ethereal like your gloves, but each time I actively use it, tappin' it with my ki

The Generalist

skills, it takes up a charge - it only holds three charges per 24 hours before recharging naturally, solar-powered nonetheless! The charges last up to five minutes though, so I gotta make it count. But yeah, 'cuz of how much strength I can wield, you've never been able to find the right materials or a bat custom-made properly enough to take more than three charges. Trust me, you've tried!"

"So you can't just make ANYTHING into an Artifact?" I asked, running my fingers through my bangs, setting them to the side of my ear.

"No, you can make any object, item, or artifact into an Object, Item, or Artifact. You hear them capitalized letters? That's 'cuz they've been upgraded through the power of Artificing, an art form as you called it. You can make even something as everyday and ordinary as a pen, a simple object, into an Artifact...but because of the nature of the base materials, you can only do so much with it. You can never make a simple object into an Artifact that can, say, give you Troll Regeneration, right? But you can easily do a pen that can change colors just by tapping into it with a small shot of energy. You can make a pen that will never smudge or take your fingerprints, by activating it. Or you can make a pen that is nothing but a gigantic beacon, radiating the energy of your choice and traceable by you alone - that's one of your favorite techniques when it comes to tracking people, y'know.

Taboo 0: Cliché of Memories

An artifact that is raised to the status of Artifact is the most powerful of all, composed of only the best materials to be found and already kinda imbued with powers of its own. Hell, that's basically how you made the Ghosthunter wooden sword - you didn't transform it into an Artifact until you hunted down and exorcised a thousand demons with the damn thing, all 'Fallen Thrones' nonetheless! 'Cept now it's so freakin' powerful you can't use the thing without it activating your...uh, thingy. Don't look at me like that - I honestly can't tell you 'bout it, or your abilities, or you'll accidentally activate it simply by knowing of its existence."

"For real? It's like that, huh?" I frowned, thinking this was something I had obviously prepared my partner for ahead of time.

"Hell yeah for real. You always told me that if you lost your memories, got personality-swapped, somehow got Alzheimers, or even got mindwiped or chakra-blasted, that I should let you know that if you actively became aware of certain abilities, you might activate them and blow everything the hell up. Best you don't ask 'bout 'em, I won't talk. There's also letters and shit you left yourself, a whole book of 'em, and journals, right? Like you always said boss, be prepared! BUT, I can't just show them to you – either you'll feel the drive to find them on yer own or ya won't."

The Generalist

I frowned at that, something he said earlier prickled at the back of my mind as he sang loudly along with the radio, intent on the road. I knew instinctively that there were three types of demons: the classical biblical ones and the interdimensional travelers who didn't belong on this dimension, but for the life of me I couldn't remember what the final type were, and I knew VERY instinctively that they were the worst, most powerful types, able to cause death and destruction on all four realms simultaneously simply by their existence and the nature of their strength.

But what were they, and why did I know so instinctively how bad they were...?

*****

Taboo 0: Cliché of Memories
Round 4

The Hold itself was relatively small, considering the importance of the cutting to their religion. The apartment complex was set in a square fashion, and only once they entered the central courtyard did it make more sense: a tree, larger than anything I could remember, grew in the center of the courtyard, taking up much of the garden space. The branches spread out, reaching up for sunlight even as he somehow knew the roots grew further down than a normal tree should, not simply absorbing inasmuch as it was cycling the energies and nutrients to be found therein. This was the cutting of Yggdrasil, the greatest treasure to the Asture and their reason for being.

Closing my gaping jaw, I noted Dash's slight head nod towards the tree before doing the same, feeling awestruck by the beauty and majesty of the thing. Shit, it GLOWED, y'know? Like, freakin' glowed. On some other level, I could feel the edges of my perception begin to itch again. Something about the tree was sincerely messing with the edges of my vision, and a palpable sense of something seeking about the edges of my perception, poking here and there, overcame me. For a moment I took a step back and could feel the...the...something, back off completely, and I was left shaking internally.

What the fuck was THAT?!

The Generalist

Then the biggest dude I've ever seen (so far as I remember) ambled around the trunk of that powerful tree, and I was struck once again that I haven't EVER been in Kansas. A "normal" life apparently just had never been in the cards for me. The dude wasn't big the way Dash was (all shoulders and limbs), but seriously huge - he was both tall and wide at the same time, and wore a simple brown robe that covered him from thick, bullish neck to the tops of his feet. I could see comfortable-looking slippers peeking out from under the robe, and overall he didn't give an air of obesity or muscle. I honestly couldn't tell if he was powerful or just a butterball, and the air about him gave me enough consideration that I really REALLY didn't want to find out!

In his left hand he held a branch; not a staff, a freakin' branch, though from what I could tell the ends had never seen a blade. As he lifted up a hand to touch the trunk of the entity (can it really be called a tree?!) a series of red glowing runic glyphs flowed out from the trunk itself in a band, lifting away from the tree for a moment before fading. The sensation that I was being watched faded along with the runes and the ginormo dude cleared his throat with a rumble. Now that I wasn't as shocked by the sheer immensity of him, I was able to note the ruddy, clean peach-color of his skin, where I could see it on his face - not only was he himself humongous, but his freakin' BEARD, man!

Taboo 0: Cliché of Memories

It was...it was phenomenal! Where beard, mustache, and hair met I could hardly tell, and indeed it seemed to be a thing all of its own.

This. This was the beard of a true wizard, man!

I didn't care about the rest of his face (piercingly intelligent green eyes, the generous mouth, or the strangely slender ears that peeked out from underneath his wild matting of hair that flowed out from behind that glorious beard), but man...that facial hair!

Did I mention this was the look of a true wizard? I stopped gaping at his beard the moment his rumbling voice cleared my senses and pissed me off.

"It's about time. She's still got your gloves. Ass."

...wait, did I want to kill this guy before I lost my memories? Because I suddenly wanted to kill this fucking guy.

Halting my oncoming growl, Dash merely laughed at the challenging tone, "Hey Abby! Yeah, did Vee tell you 'bout Franky boy?"

"Yeah, he's in trouble. As always. And is going to try to get my wife in trouble. As always. And the name is Abbacus, troll. Abbacus Keith, of the proud Norse Keith family."

The Generalist

Did I mention things just got really complicated, what with this guy being the Priestess's husband? 'Cuz things got really, REALLY complicated in a New York freakin' minute! Unsure of my stance with the guy I stayed quiet, realizing he had been watching me since he first showed up. I cleared my own throat nervously, unsure of what to do next when Dash once again saved me.

"Yeah, I know Abba. Hey, can we skip the formalities? And stop freakin' Frank out, he'll probably remember this shit and get you back for it after he gets his memories back, y'know," Dash looked about, "Where's Vee anyway?"

I then let out a relieved breath as 'Abby' suddenly chuckled and his entire being seemed to relax, the joke suddenly bursting. It then dawned on me that the Priestess had warned him ahead of time about my condition and he was having fun at my expense - at least I had a better idea of where I stood with him as he chuckled harder, "Oh, oh you bastard. Daniel, if I can't have fun at my friend's and comrade's expense, what purpose is there to life? We're done taking petitioners for the day, so she's in the bath. You stay here. Frank can go and approach her, if he dares."

There, that glinting look in his light green eyes caught my attention and it suddenly dawned on me that this was perhaps the nature of our relationship, as bros. But was

Taboo 0: Cliché of Memories

that the hint of a challenge I suspected in his warm, even tones? The bastard.

   I drew myself up and immediately walked forward, only for a strangely slender hand to fall upon my shoulder. I looked askance at him and noted those hands; they weren't like my own or Dash's blunt instruments of death, but artistic, fingers meant for playing piano, but skilled nonetheless in interesting strikes.

   "You're going the wrong way, Frank. Apartment 4C is where the Priestess's Bath is…," he chuckled, that look in his eyes hinting challenge again. So, the challenge wasn't WHERE it was, but if I had the balls to go or not, "…where you'll find Priestess Vorel, post-duties."

   Once again puffing myself up, I walked with my back straight and my head held high, certain the Frank Todd of pre-memory loss would've done so as well. Ignoring Dash's catcalls and whistles, I headed to Apartment 4C (third floor, to the west of the courtyard) and at first reached for the doorknob only to hesitate, suddenly overcome with the feeling that I shouldn't.

   I did NOT look back though. I squared my shoulders, touched the doorknob, ignored everything (and I do mean everything) and opened the door, stepping into the room while still ignoring everything.

   That. Did not. Last long.

The Generalist

Diaphanous silks hung from the ceiling and against the walls, screwing with my vision - that and the hazy, tangible smoke obscuring most of the forms in the dark, converted bath. Candles, melting on ornate holders and stands, cast dark shadows all about, and though I couldn't see much of the room itself and the dark forms within it I could make out various bits of furniture. The apartment itself really had been converted into one huge room, one huge Lodge - halfway through the apartment the real bath itself began, and I could spot rose petals and other flowers floating on the top of the dark waters.

My tunnel vision obliterated, I inhaled deeply of the smoke and realized what was going on - pheromones, heavy and languid in the air, began to infiltrate beyond my active defenses and my brain lit on fire, going beyond the usual itchiness into a full-blown firestorm. Through the sublime pain of it all, of something within me awakening beyond my control, I saw through everything here. Every single detail, of the naked people rising from the divans and lounging chairs, disengaging from one another to direct their attention to me.

Gods. Every last one of them had a god in their eyes, gazing at me, a challenger, one who would not fall to the pheromones, to fall into their embrace.

To be sacrificed to them, even for a little while.

Taboo 0: Cliché of Memories

And the worst part of it all was the feeling that this wasn't the first time this had happened to me, that the Frank Todd I was before the loss of my memories also found this unworthy of me. Us. In the back of my mind I could feel a power growing, something that burned brighter than the flames that were engulfing my brain, and my Voice growled, strangely synchronized with my will for the first time since waking up. This was more than just a Bath for the goddesses that lay within their shared avatar, but a chance for the Norse pantheon and their allies themselves to take on flesh and simply be themselves, enjoying the splendors of the flesh beyond their own godhoods.

And I just crashed that party.

Whether they simply wanted me to join in or to destroy me had yet to be seen, caught in the bacchanalia as they were.

Centering myself and my Voice simultaneously (what HAD to be through hours of training, this shit wouldn't've gone down otherwise!), I began to walk forward, ignoring the seeking hands and the lips reaching out to beg, to offer, to demand. Fingers plucked at my clothes but I remained generally unmolested as I walked about the petitioners, playthings of their sensation-starved gods, their flesh being ridden to appease the hungers of their deities.

The Generalist

And at the center of it all, at the far end of the Bath, she lay. Her.

Freya smiled at me wickedly, her luscious lips beckoning even as her blue eyes glared at me from Vorel's eyes turned fully black. I had walked through the trap, but that was merely the initial stages of this challenge, and as I stood before the tiled edges of the Bath I glared back at her, my brain on fire.

She lounged, her luscious body submerged within the dark waters of the netherworld that ebbed and flowed within the divine Bath, my gloves floating in the air behind her as she leaned back against the edge of the Bath itself, her arms to either side to give her purchase. Wiggling Vee's toes at me, she beckoned to me with a crook of her finger - an unmistakable gesture, a challenge and a threat, a promise and a welcoming motion all rolled into one.

Clenching and unclenching my fists, I dared to lock eyes with the ancient being within the Priestess and I realized what was going on here. A bit of flotsam, an unnecessary tidbit of information suddenly flitted across my brain and my Voice gave it word.

"For a mortal to touch the waters of the Netherworld is to know Death, Frank," my Voice informed me, knowing that bit of information as I did, *"This isn't a place for us.*

Taboo 0: Cliché of Memories

We're not Asture, nor are we protected by their gods! Their pantheon protects them during this affirmation of their connection, of their power. They give their bodies to their gods and those gods protect them - what do we have?"

"*Faith,*" I thought back to the Voice, "*Faith in ourselves. We've done this before, I can freakin' taste it. We've probably done this a lot. All I know is that we need those Gloves, and apparently Freya won't let us get them without passing this challenge. Fine then. Let's do work, kid.*"

I centered myself, thinking about what Frank Todd would do. By all accounts and by everything I've seen and read thus far, he would just take the next step, then another, all the while remembering who and what he was.

So that's what I did. After all, memories or not, I WAS Frank Todd!

The ever-lovin' Generalist!

So I took the first step and immediately nearly jumped, barely catching myself as lines of red, glowing runes erupted from the tiles themselves in response to my own power, flaring out of control in further response to the black Netherworld waters. Waters so black, so dark that even though I could see the tiles of the bottom of the Bath with its floating red runes of power, I knew instinctively

The Generalist
that what I was looking at was an illusion.

There was no bottom. There was no bottom to the Bath, the place where the playthings of the gods made sport.

Yet as I stepped down, I kept within my mind the unwavering image of the man I had been, the man I had read about. The man I was.

The man I was going to hopefully be once again.

And with both myself and the Voice in my head focusing on that alone, we took the first step and touched the bottom of the Bath, the waters parting under our boot as if I was Moses and it was the Red Sea. I took a further step, burning with energy, glowing with power, and the dark waters receded further before me and stayed apart behind me, unwilling or unable to touch me as I kept focused and centered on the one thing.

I was Frank Todd and as God as my fuckin' witness, I was going to get my gloves back from this beautiful goddess!!!

Step by step I made my way slowly to her, sauntering almost, my chocolate brown eyes burning with the acceptance of this challenge. The goddess, at first strong in her Bath, strong within the waters of the Netherworld, was indeed as haughty and confident as a creature such as She had every right to be. As I drew closer though the

Taboo 0: Cliché of Memories

look in her eyes began to change and she realized that I wasn't going to fall as easily as she had predicted.

Rising to her feet she waved her arm once and three ornate, glowing spears suddenly slammed up out of the ground to bar my path, one directly in front of me and two more criss-crossing it. Snarling I reached up with my right, gloved hand and grasped the closest spear by the shaft, eliciting a gasp from the onlookers of the Bath as it began to crumple in my hand. I never questioned how I got my gloves back on, nor how I was able to hold onto such a divine weapon, only keeping in mind who I was and what I was. Grasping it and throwing it aside I reached up with my left, gloved hand and did it again to the second spear, then gripped the third spear with both hands and tore it into two, the muscles of my body electric with strength and power.

Taking the last four steps towards the goddess, I finally allowed myself to pant and grin like the bastard I was, the goddess panting beautifully before me at the expenditure of her power.

"Will you even now deny me worship, Frank? Do both of you deny me then?"

Her voice was small and plaintive within my mind, and it damn near broke my heart to see the hurt that lay behind those proud eyes of her. It then dawned on me that I was

The Generalist

not only in love with the Priestess herself, but perhaps the goddesses that lay within her as their avatar. Reaching beyond her I drew a towel around her strong shoulders and began to rub at her arms, my eyes never straying from her despite how delectable her body was, how much I wanted to take her right then and there.

"Naw. We love you, all of you. Right?" I asked my Voice.

I could practically feel the Voice nodding in my head as it intoned back, *"Yeah! All four of ya, y'know? You're all in there like I am, you know how it goes. "*

Though the goddess sighed in consternation, Vorel wore a small smile as she leaned against me, purring as I dried her off before murmuring, "You're not fully Frank yet. You're not my Thomas yet. You have the gloves you desire, and you have pleased us by being the main spectacle of the night. We have been entertained and though you still do not bow to us, we-!"

Her breath suddenly hitched as I fell to one knee, taking her hand in both of mine. The pantheon of gods, watching, realized they had been caught unawares by my move and it dawned on me that while I may have been flirting with disaster that this was the right move to make.

"Well, since you like us so much, I won't promise myself to you guys...but perhaps you'll accept the promise

Taboo 0: Cliché of Memories

of us comin' back sometime to entertain you guys again?" I kissed the palm of her hand, watching with delight as she shivered, the very air around us charged with a tangible power, as if my words were somehow working reality itself to my whim, "This was interesting, in the very least, and I think you'd like me better with my full memories."

Turning with a wave, I strode out of the Bath confidently, the tinkling laughter of the goddess following me as I left still in her favor, still with her love.

****

An hour later, I realized this was pretty much Frank Todd's life. My life. The life of The Generalist. Dizzying highs, terrifying lows, all juxtaposed to one another, one always immediately following the other.

While I left all smiles and all badassed and what-not, I immediately fell into a depression as Dash and I jumped into The Roadbuster and the troll turned to me and happily intoned, "And NOW for the Vatican Warlock Assassins!"

Ever since then I pretty much just laid listlessly against the passenger window, at times scratching at the window and screaming to be let out. Man, I bet this was how manic-depressive bipolars felt.

The Generalist

Ohhhhhhh boy. I did NOT want to go through with this!

"I mean c'mon, I got the gloves! I got the flask! What else are we supposed to do? I'm not even me right now, I'm still...uh, me without memories!!!" I whined pathetically as Dash rolled his eyes and for the umpteenth time told me those words I was growing to hate.

"You're Frank Todd, bro. Just do what you do. Activate the gloves, whup some ass, find out why they want that flask Artifact so bad and what they did to your memories. Get your memories back. Be awesome. It's what we do, brother!"

"But I don't KNOW how to activate the gloves~!" I whined again, feeling like I had somehow left my balls back at the Bath, "I don't even know how I did that stuff back there, I just went up to the hot naked lady and had my gloves back, y'know? I didn't even fuckin' put 'em on! They were just on! LET ME OUTTA HERE!"

And so the conversation went on until we finally reached our destination: Venice Beach. Under the cover of darkness we parked on the boardwalk and I noted the time as being 1 a.m., realizing how full of a day it had been for me with or without memories.

"The true Witching time," my Voice said unhelpfully, feeling as down as I did about this. Still, we were me...uh, I was me, and taking a deep breath I centered myself and

Taboo 0: Cliché of Memories

got out of the car and gazed about the place, feeling a part of me scanning about for life while I and my Voice simply enjoyed the scenery. Now first, imagine if you will a wonderfully moonlit beach (a full moon nonetheless!), a boardwalk, all kinds of closed down shops and the sound of the surf being pounded by the waves. It was a good night to be on the beach, yet there wasn't a soul to be found, making the entire scene surreal, almost breathtaking in its other-worldliness.

   Then the streetlights began to go out one by one, from the distant horizon and drawing closer with each streetlight that blew out. With each streetlight that died my anxiety began to ramp up, and as the darkness stretched out to embrace us both I realized that this so-called meeting under the flag of truce had just broke out into a full-scale fight!

   I backed up into open space as Dash roared, grabbing The Roadbuster by the Whammy Bar and yanking her in front of us and setting her onto her side as well, the car body and chassis beginning to glow as lines upon lines of ornate glyphs erupted into golden light, driving back the darkness. The darkness, apparently having none of that, instead encircled our lonely streetlight and began to blow out the rest down the boardwalk, plunging us into a cocoon of absolute pitch black, the streetlight overhead and The Roadbuster being our only light.

The Generalist

"Why are we fighting them again?!" I thought back to the strange phone call he had made to the Vatican, at first snarling and yelling but soon placated by someone who called himself Father Schlaket.

"Because they're Catholics!" the troll grunted, then considered for a moment while looking about into the darkness, "and they're assass-AW HELL! FRANK! TIME TO DO IT! I CAN SMELL THAT SPELL GETTIN' CHARGED!!" Dash smiled at me with that maniacal grin and I gasped in horror as his features suddenly grew...trollier. Nothing changed save that his green eyes now glowed with an almost laser-like red, bright and angry with battlelust, yet that one small detail suddenly threw his entire visage from the comfortably human face I had grown used to with him into an absolute monster.

He barked with laughter, "C'MON, DO THAT THING AND LET'S PUT FIST TO FACE!"

"But...I still don't know what to do!" This time I wasn't whining, I just wasn't READY for this!

Dash frowned, "Wait, what? Dude, this is their standard operating procedure - Darkness Embrace to fuck up their target's sense of the environment, followed by a charged spell! Probably Solar Litany or somethin' in a conical or line formation! Dude, you OH GOD I FORGOT YOU HAVE THAT MEMORY LOSS THING!"

Taboo 0: Cliché of Memories

The troll grunted and settled himself behind the car, holding it at (long) arms length as the darkness suddenly faded away, the moon above providing more than enough illumination alongside the orb that burned damn near in front of us.

Three dark-clothed gents, sturdy black slippers on their feet, stood behind the orb, the one in the middle chanting from an opened Bible while the other two had their hands towards each other on either side of the orb, strange energies flowing from all three to meld with the burning orb as it grew larger. They each wore the same thing: a black duster buttoned up over crimson button-up shirts with a white priest's color at each neck, black slacks and a strange, crimson cloth mask concealing their faces, a triangular hat perched atop each head with a long braid that they had over their shoulders.

Dash roared and I saw an equally strange energy erupt somewhere within his chest and course through his arms, touching The Roadbuster and mingling with the glyphs that glowed about her, changing the color from the fierce gold into a greenish light.

Putting my shoulder to the car I decided to trust in both Dash and the car - I helped make this thing, and I was fairly certain Frank Todd was the kind of guy to not do things half-assed!

The Generalist

"Don't forget what you've learned here tonight, Todd," the Runesmith had told me before we left, his last bit of advice flying through my skull, *"that no matter what, ultimately you are you. You have proven this to us time and time again and, even without your memories, you are still you. Trust in that, as we do, and go with the gods my friend."*

The two warlock assassins slumped slightly, their hands glued to the brightly burning orb of flame. The third added his own hands to the spell, the Bible burning up and scattering into ash as all three began to chant that strange nonsense, their energies co-mingling and activating the spell.

Then it happened: our defenses versus their siege.

The orb flashed once then exploded forth, pouring itself out in a relentless torrent, a single bar of white-hot golden flame of divine magic, smashing against The Roadbuster, the energies crashing against one another, finding purchase anywhere they could. The troll, his boots digging furrows into the ground, roared in pain as the shockwave of energy cascaded THROUGH us, the damage of the spell itself buffered by The Roadbuster's innate defenses but the energy itself still coursing about us. I heard someone screaming and did my level best to shut the fuck up, realizing the screamer was me. Shivering, I looked over to Dash as the troll crashed to one knee, his muscles

Taboo 0: Cliché of Memories

rippling as he held up the bulwark of our defense.

"Frank...FRANK! You've...gotta do it now, bro!" Dash leaned back, then roared and hurtled himself forward, setting his shoulder against the car from his kneeling position, "I can't take much more of this! You've GOT to do it!"

"Do WHAT?! I can't do anything!!!!" I wanted to help. I wanted to help! I wanted to help Dash, but...what could I do?

How did I do it?! These weird energies, glowing auras and this world of magic and monsters.

This wasn't the real world! This had to be a fucked-up dream!

I wanted to help, I wanted to be helped, I was...I was...

"YES, you can! You're the fuckin' Generalist, man!" Dash began to falter, driven to both knees under their assault and I saw the energy beginning to surge from him even as he took more damage, his trollish regeneration taking hold but not enough, nowhere near fast enough! "You're Frank Todd!"

Amidst the swirling energies of the various magics, ki, psionic energy and spiritual power I leaped. I leaped over the car and through the flames even as they burned at my

The Generalist

clothes, at my soul, my hands burning from the Maximum Gloves, the Artifacts reacting actively to my choice.

I hurtled myself forward automatically and without thinking, grabbing at the edge of the car's undercarriage to do so.

Ignoring the heat, the flames.

Ignoring the pain, the rush of inevitably certain death.

Ignoring everything except for the sudden realization.

I WAS Frank Todd! And the one thing Frank Todd did, the secret to everything, suddenly opened up to me and in that instant I knew what to do. The ancient covenant, held deep within me, suddenly reignited:

Define yourself
Break yourself
Hate yourself
Become all

The Generalist

Within me screamed the flames of my own energies as they surged to the fore, soaring through me.

Outside of me, the flames of my enemies, the surging of their fire as it burned around my shield, my armor.

I reveled in the rush of hatred and energy, fueled by my rage, as my multi-layered defenses activated automatically. The Brick Wall erupted before me. My plate-like Armor surged around me, refracted with the black color of my aura. The Bubble appeared about me, then a thousand more, each one weaker than the last but requiring a new attack to destroy each one, each one demanding and disrupting the energies of the Solar Litany spell.

And at the heart of it all my memories erupted through me, empowering me, my Empathy devouring it all, and in a mad rush I activated my Overdrive, the divine gift of absolute dread, my abilities and strengths rising to new, inhuman heights as they worked faster, harder, and more efficiently than before.

I was one of the Five Survivors.

I was one of the heroes of the Fall of Perris.

I was one of the few men who had dared to glare back at the eyes of gods and behold the spectacle every time they did so, my will absolute in its strength.

Taboo 0: Cliché of Memories

I was the goddamned Generalist. I was Frank Todd.

And this was MY fucking city!!!!

Snarling, the energies of the spell ripping through the thin Bubbles I had placed around my aura, I blinked and immediately entered into Psycho Space, the three brightly flaring auras before me revealing everything about the targets even as the self that was my Aura spun and hurtled three Hookshots into them, the psychic manifestation of infiltration into another's soul, the connection of one will to another. The three ribbons of myself, tipped as they were with blades that no sword could parry, immediately sank into the heart chakra of all three assassins and the spell immediately faltered and stopped, their concentration completely broken as they attempted to scramble back into the cover of darkness.

But the darkness was magical in origin, and as I saw the magical energy they poured forth from their auras to feed the spell I synchronized myself to them with a surge of psionic power and forced the spell back onto their own eyes, temporarily blinding all three – a good trick if you understood the natures of both spiritual power and magically-based energy and how they worked together. You cannot synchronize with a magical source, but spiritual people tend to leave themselves open when cross-casting – thus leaving themselves open to be synchronized with instead.

The Generalist

Blinking again, my vision changed and I was back on the boardwalk of Venice Beach, the three assassins screaming in terror as they clawed at their own faces, rolling about or trying to crawl away. I frowned at them and realized I overdid it a little, re-adjusting my Maximum Gloves and checking that they were properly empowered once again.

The fight wasn't over though. The effects of the blinding weren't permanent unless I performed the proper binding ritual, and all I HAD on me were my damn gloves! And the flask.

Remembering what my mission for this was, I began to reach for the flask when I heard Dash's voice ring out at the same time as my Voice, "LOOK OUT!"

Shifting my attention back, I realized one of the assassins (Vatican Warlock Assassins, Jesus spare me) had already gone into a battle trance in order to counter the effects of the blindness. Spinning through the air, the assassins foot flickered out several times, intent on my vitals - a quick turn to evade the attack and a hard clothesline brought that mess to a screeching halt, employing just a little bit of telekinesis in order to slam the priest even harder into the ground.

What I did, instead, was accidentally send the man through the boardwalk itself, crashing into the sand below

Taboo 0: Cliché of Memories

as I put a little too much oomph into it, my brain and gut warming comfortably from the exertion. Even more memories came crashing into me and I FINALLY remembered my full esper training, both under my parents and with the Skinwalker unit in the Army.

Flexing my fist, I grinned and turned to Dash, on his knees and panting behind Rhonda, "Hey bro, you doin' good?"

The troll merely waved, his big hands visible over the side of the car as his regeneration began to kick back in, stunned as it was by the wave of spiritual-magic energy. Chuckling, I turned back to figure out how best to deal with the other two assassins.

Stumbling about, one of them shook his head and noticed me but all too late - before he could react I had taken up a baseball pitcher's position, eyeing him before hurtling a ball of combined telekinetic and ki energy directly at his face. The man cart-wheeled through the air before slamming into a streetlight, toppling the damn thing before slumping down.

Hells yes, my Fastball still had that whopping hit!

Spinning to the side, I narrowly dodged a fast jump kick from the third assassin, crouching lightly into his guard as I did so. The assassin, his cloth mask torn and rent enough for me to see his face (not a handsome face, but not a plain

The Generalist

one either - the Catholics sure did know how to pick 'em!) and the look of surprise on it. I had lucked out, figuring out that while they were able to employ spiritual faith, magical energy, and ki energy they hadn't a clue about psionics - I was still Hookshotted into 'em, able to feel their emotions, intent, and even thoughts so long as they didn't brush it off or take it out.

Grinning up at the surprised choir boy, I immediately rose and slammed the palm of my hand into his face, gripping it hard at the temples and letting the Gloves do their thing. The greatest of my Artifacts, the gloves did more than simply amplify the energies I manipulated within my inner-verse and immediate outer-verse, but also improved my grip strength and overall physical prowess. That, combined with the Overdrive, and I could've pulped the guy's head with one twitch of my hand.

Instead I felt I needed a little vindication for what had happened that night. It had been a long day, I was cranky, and this guy was one of the three rebels who sought to create their own cult with the aid of the ancient artifact that now warmed my back pocket, alongside the blood of the troll.

The troll who was counted amongst my closest of friends.

And with THAT all noted I let loose with my full esper

Taboo 0: Cliché of Memories

power, my quirk of an ability draining the man completely of all emotions, burning out the parts of his mind and aura that produced both emotions and the ability to produce the chemicals they were associated with, my fifth and eighth chakra flaring brightly as I gorged on his emotions, content with just that instead of his whole freakin' existence.

At first he struggled, gripping at my wrists, clawing at my chest, doing whatever he could do to stop me from doing this horrible thing to him. He called upon God many times, screaming at times as I devoured his memories.

But I was pissed, and God was the client who had hired me to recover the Artifact, an ancient one of Its very own design from back in the day, and deliver these guys to Its "boys" to begin with.

Eventually the priest stopped moving, at first little by little then worse. Frowning distastefully I let go of the vegetable, watching dispassionately as he fell to his knees then toppled over, his eyes open but without sight as his head hit the ground – a human without emotions, and the chemicals that were associated with them. He was alive though, all three of them were as was part of the deal.

God hated rogue factions in Its church, but It hated those who broke contracts even further.

Still, NO ONE did this to me, to my friend, and got

The Generalist

away with it easy. And God said It wanted them alive, and had purposefully left out whether or not they were to be cerebrally intact.

Channeling the men's emotions and memories into the thirsty Artifact (which had been devouring any and all liquids and energies about me the entire time), I patted the flask and put it back into my back pocket, unhooking myself empathically from the three would-be godlings as Dash righted The Roadbuster, our baby, back onto all four wheels.

"Aw man, the paint! Hey, Frank...you Frank again?"

I turned and grinned at him, giving him a thumbs-up, "Yeap! I'm back, baby!"

"Good! Then this time YOU pay for the fucking paint job!"

****

Taboo 0: Cliché of Memories
Round 5

It was 3 a.m. by the time the Vatican had sent their usual fix-it team, ensuring that the environment was once again back to the pristine pre-fight looks it had sported before we wrecked it. By then I had ramped my Overdrive back down to its weakest settings, but even then I could feel it humming in the background of my various powers and abilities, ever and always unable to completely shut off.

Ergo why my life was such a wreck most of the time: we Five Survivors of the Fall of Perris had gained these abilities, but they all had the absolute con of attracting demonic attention while activated.

Unlike the other four, though, the Overdrive could never be shut off. So my life was always exciting, always being bothered by such creatures sniffing me out the moment they got near my aura.

And ladies and gentlemen, lemme tell you I have QUITE the aura!

Ignoring Dash's plaintive yelps about wanting to drive, I drove us to Lucky's, our favorite diner, in fact the one I fled from earlier. Nodding to the cute blonde waitress (bubbly, bouncy, petite and always fun) I took up our resident seat by the bar, ignoring the tables and patrons as

The Generalist

a portly, graying man simply flickered into the seat next to me. At one blink he wasn't there, then I blinked and he was there, apparently having put his ski-ball on hold until the mission was over...and also having the bad luck of losing my visage as he ran across THIS guy again.

Other deities would've probably come in with all sorts of fanfare and special effects (except for Odin – he was so austere he was downright rocky...if it wasn't for his strong love of bad jokes), but that was how God liked to operate, after all. No flair for the dramatic, this one - all the jazz and glamor of Its profession was put in as an afterthought by King James, Its favorite and most bitter target of argument.

"And rightfully it should be, Franky boy! James had no backbone, was manipulated by Peter's church, and screwed up what should've been my bestselling magnus opus! I'm tellin' ya, they get you in the editing department, they do!"

I chuckled and continued to drink my coffee, glad I was able to have the damn thing after the long evening had finally ended. Without saying a word I passed the flask to God who made it disappear with a flourish and a flick of Its wrist, the deal now done. Though I never requested payment I knew the Vatican would secretly wire a sizable donation to the Brownstone group, the organization that handled all of my banking needs. In truth, the Brownstone

Taboo 0: Cliché of Memories

group was a front for the Scarletti family, the mafia of monsters I worked for part-time as a loan shark. That didn't stop them from being honestly one of the best financial and investment groups out there, though, and that's why we ultimately bank with them.

Hey, don't look at me like that about the loan shark side of The Shop. It's a freakin' living, and even monster-genes need a hand up, not a handout. We were ethical in how we treated our customers, and always gave them every opportunity to pay us back without going bankrupt or taking food away from the table. Rent always got paid with The Shop, and that's the motto we live by.

"This was a tricky one, it was. To think, they wanted this trinket without paying the proper tolls, huh! Thankfully you've got energy to spare, or this trinket would've drained you of your aura, spirit, and blood! And to think they honestly thought they could handle it and gain its power. Start their own cult! From my flock!!!" God pounded on the bar for a moment, breaking it and fixing it at the same time. It rubbed at Its gloved hand, Its skin starting to take on the familiar brown coloration of my own and I realized It was doing it again, preparing to slander my good name (or what was left of it) all over town with Its' scandalous activities.

Still, it also helped me out in the long run as I grew in infamy and good karma. Ultimately it balanced out, and

The Generalist

that's all that mattered to me. Chuckling I ordered another cup of coffee for both of us, "So, Yahweh...what ARE you going to do about the other Artifact they used to try and neutralize me? Memory-wipes are strictly against the Pact, y'know."

God glared at me with my own eyes, Its body only now beginning to transform to mimic mine, unable to simply do so at a faster pace now that I was in control of my faculties again - being truly aware of It slowed down Its' ability to take on your guise, "What memory wipe? You're you, aren't you? Kitty took care of that, and now the Artifact exists no longer. Oy, what kind of a schmendrick do you take me for, eh? Pact-schmact."

I sipped at my coffee, paying the waitress early as was my wont. God might've been a shyster, but It was legit when it came to deals so long as you caught him early enough. Indeed, the Artifact probably DID no longer exist, but I'd still check with my Catholic contacts (Father Gustav Hunden Von Schlaket, the "Hound of Slaughter") and the FBI (Agent Mesmer, bah what a naming scheme they had) to make sure he didn't pull a fast one.

Speaking about naming schemes I thought on Kitty, the name the Voice in my head had chosen upon his creation so many years ago.

I rubbed at my temple, thinking on how that trio of

Taboo 0: Cliché of Memories

annoying assassins had tricked me into meeting under a false flag of truce and I, like a moron, had thought to take advantage of the situation and try something new out. The whole shenanigans that had occurred afterward had proven my theory that Kitty, the second soul that resided within me, could indeed create a psychic partition within me, like a black box, that could only be opened at a time of great need. I should've realized that he would've connected it to our sense of loyalty, our need to protect our friends and each other, but this one had been a close one! If I hadn't've stumbled across Dash (who admitted to only finding me on accident) earlier today, I probably would've still been walking around looking for a goddamn phone book in this god-stuffed town.

"Sorry," Kitty apologized to me inside of our head, hugging me, *"Had I thought it out a bit better-"*

"No, no," I apologized back to Kitty, patting his hands...er, so to speak, *"It was my bad. I'm always expounding on the nature of loyalty and such, and you know how dear our friends are to us."*

Besides, they had plans to bond the flask to Dash, using him like a perpetual sacrifice engine or some shit. If I had drained the first guy and learned that, God might've gotten three corpses instead of the living bodies we gave It.

"Yer damn right, and a fine job of it you did!" My twin

The Generalist

grinned at me with a familiar bastard grin, patting down Its afro before getting off the bar stool, "And we have GOT to stop meeting at diners like this! All night diners always make me hungry, and this isn't my part of town - time to amscray out before this body shifts again, yeah? Until next time, Todd."

I held my cup up in salutations, "*Vaya con Dios*, Dios!"

God turned around with my body and grinned at me, making two pistol motions with thumb and forefinger in my direction, "*Vaya con* Me, Franky boy!"

With that I watched God amble out and immediately put Its arms around two women, whispering sweet nothings in their ears and already making promises It was going to weasel out of in a pseudo-honorable fashion. I chuckled good-naturedly: I really dug that guy, but MAN did the books lie 'bout It!

"Hey, Frank," I opened my eyes and looked over at Laura, wondering if she was going to reprimand me for looking too mean again. Instead she offered me a cup of water and a pretty smile, "You look like you could use a little conversation after your friend left. Wanna hang out and chat?"

Chat. Huh. I wouldn't even know where to begin, the two of us from completely different worlds no matter how entrenched within mine she was. But here at Lucky's,

Taboo 0: Cliché of Memories

everyone was the same - it's why I enjoyed this place so much. After a long while of bad jokes and using every trick to ham up my story in order to earn a smile from her I finally realized how early it was and yawned, excusing myself and prepared to leave. For a moment I could sense a flash of disappointment from the pretty waitress before she once again graced me with that smile of hers, and I felt a small twinge of regret.

"If you want, I'll pop around again tomorrow," I grinned slightly, "Hell, I'll even bring a coupla friends, get this place jumpin' at 3 a.m., yeah?"

She nodded, her blonde ponytail bobbing energetically, "Sounds good, Frank! Remember, you promised, yeah?"

I chuckled and took my leave, returning her wave as I thought back to the tidbit of information God had helped us unlock during our conversation on the Physical Plane, buckling myself into The Roadbuster in order to replay those memories in my head.

The three assassins had jumped me and wiped my head, just as planned. But what happened afterwards wasn't.

I could still taste his strange energy about me as Morrow Kind, one of the five survivors of the Fall of Perris, appeared in a flash of long blonde hair, fighting off the assassins with his strange musical magics and martial arts. Small and beautiful, yet the older man had carried me

The Generalist

to that condo in his arms as if I weighed nothing, even though I was damn near twice his size in muscle and height.

He was the one who had filled the bathtub with blood in order to placate the Artifact (an Artifact that is anchored to your energy signature means that YOU have to pay the toll if there is one, even if it's not on your person physically), and if it wasn't for that I probably would've been far weaker throughout the entire night. I also wasn't going to look too closely at where he got the blood, either.

Morrow Kind, with the gray eye he was born with and one violet eye, gained the same day I gained the Overdrive. He of the long blonde hair, too impossibly soft to be a man's, his figure far too feminine to be as strong as it was. Though Aquarius, the violin he had used during the Fall, was safely locked away in the Armory he was still a force to be reckoned with, able to simply hum in order to utilize the strange, otherworldly energies that made up his aura. He had also gone missing damn near completely after the Fall of Perris, his name becoming only a whispered rumor within the various circles we traveled, a fact that caused the various worldwide governments all sorts of trouble.

"And should any of the Five be too close to one another for longer than thirty hours, what they had sealed away that day could come back!"

Taboo 0: Cliché of Memories

With that thought I closed my eyes and extended my aura as far as it would go, covering the entirety of what was basically "my land," the lion's share of Los Angeles that was mine to patrol, mine to sift through and gather emotions, intent on ensuring that Kind wasn't within my demesne.

All psionics did this, and all empaths were even more highly skilled at blanketing land with their energy signature, gathering and sampling emotions and energies from all within that land. One would think that this kinda made us vampires, 'cept we don't die if we don't do it.

But it's not without its addictive nature, and once tasted one could never go back to ever being normal. To constantly use esper abilities, as some were driven to do, was to always court Burn Out, the literal overload of one's synaptic movement and forever cauterizing the brain and the fifth chakra, the gut one.

Still, as I extended my power to the utmost limit that I ever do, I couldn't taste Morrow's strange energy signature at all. I saw Vorel, at home with her eight children as they slept, watching them carefully as one tossed about in a fit. She turned and looked up at the full moon, her ardor sated but never spent, and knew damn well what I was doing. All four, the three goddesses and their avatar, took note of where I was and allowed me to stay if I wished...

The Generalist

Dash chuckled good-naturedly as our friend, "Grease Monkey," short and Mexican and powerfully muscled, yelled at him for the damage we had done to Rhonda that night. Both turned for a moment, feeling me touch upon them, before going back to yelling and being yelled at. If Dash was her daddy, then Greasy was her grampaw, and before long the two would be fixing her up, happy and eager to improve her.

I felt Laura, nearby, preparing to close down and clean up the diner until the owner and his wife showed up to take over the breakfast shift, mulling over our conversation and chuckling to herself over a few bad jokes I had cracked. For a moment she looked directly at me with those piercing blue eyes of hers – completely fearless, she gazed dead at me before accepting that I wasn't some random ethereal, intent on going home and, as always, accepting my psionic presence as something natural.

God, as bright to me as the full moon at night, prepared Itself for a night of naughtiness, Its last night on Earth before taking off to handle Its divine responsibilities. I felt the various Pantheons as they moved their avatars about the demesne of Los Angeles and further, always and ever jockeying for higher positions of power, for more petitioners, more worship.

I felt my friends and loved ones, my beloveds, all those

Taboo 0: Cliché of Memories

who kept me anchored to Los Angeles. I felt the hatred and bitterness of beaten enemies, of many who would consider me their rival, their nemesis, and many who had been destroyed by me and my crew.

I felt Vitto Scarletti in his mansion, addressing his boys over a hit they were going to do soon. I felt Agent Mesmer as he secretly conferred with Father Gustav Von Schlaket in an abandoned warehouse somewhere downtown, the latter balking at ever approaching the American FBI for help. Mesmer was going to jockey for some clandestine funds for keeping this recent Artifact schlemping under wraps, especially since the recent budget cuts. Both pointedly ignored me, though recognized my energy pattern as I drew close.

I felt the hearts and minds and souls of all those who dwelt within my demesne, my range, and for a second those who dreamed also felt me.

I was the man in the dark. I was the boogeyman in the closet. I was Oogie fucking Boogie, ready to devour monsters and gods alike, ready to destroy any human annoying enough to bug me.

I wasn't a god.

I was just me, baby.

Just a man. Frank Todd.

The Generalist

The Generalist.

And there was one last thing for me to do....

****

Going home was always fun. I loved The Shop, as did my crew and friendlies, all of us digging on the playground we had developed together. The Shop was neutral territory for some, completely hostile ground for others, and home to quite a few. Dash and I had done tons of work, layering wave after wave of protective magics, prayers, tricks and traps, psionic glyphs and more upon the place. It was damn near an Artifact in its own right, and represented two years of hard labor to get it to this point.

Feeling the usual presence of The Shop determine who I was, a sensation that buzzed at the edges of my perception, I immediately took off my shoes and listened as someone ranted at Dash over the phone. He made the usual acknowledging noises, but ohhhhh boy was someone ripping into him! He smiled that huge, comforting smile at me as he finally got the person to calm down, made a few promising noises, then set the phone down.

Taboo 0: Cliché of Memories

"Saran wrap. Across the toilet bowl. Really, Frank? Are you fucking five years old? I can't even believe it worked! I mean, I warned him! I warned him! But Abba is honestly, seriously pissed at you!"

"Hey. You warned him I'd remember how he fucked with me while I didn't remember shit. Fuck you for laughing, fuck him for not telling me what happens at the Goddess's Bath, and fuck Alejandro Fernando for no raisin," I rubbed at my ankles with a chuckle, "I'm taking today off. Do send him a gift basket though, yeah? The usuals. He digs those fancy cheeses, man."

The troll laughed as I walked out of the Welcome Room and into The Shop, seeing it once again with eyes that understood. The harmonic resonance of the place put me at ease as I decided to fall asleep in the Library, the minor Fae flitting here and there, gently mingling the flow of the energy of the place as they carried baskets of warmth from here to there, the brownies in the walls already starting to wake up to help clean the place up wherever they found dust or dirt that wasn't an alchemical reagent. Guardians and gargoyles from outside crawled about the walls invisibly, ready to present an instant army to any who would dare come against The Shop, and the various trips, traps, backup sources of energy and more, took stock of my presence and went back to doing whatever it was they did depending on their nature.

The Generalist

A little bit of tea to calm my nerves, then sleep. Yes, despite the coffee I had. I was taking today off, but tomorrow was going to be busy as fuck. I could feel Greasy in our garage, putting the final touches to The Roadbuster, arguing with his helper spirits, both ethereal and physical, even as Dash began to also file away the last of the paperwork, eagerly intent on his hammock upstairs. My use of the Overdrive, wanton and accidental, was also going to take its toll, but thus far the physical wear and tear hadn't kicked in yet, promising pain and some time laid up as my muscles and tendons healed. Thankfully by then we'd have a new batch of Troll Brew ready, the potion I used to help my human healing system rev up and come close to a Troll-gened's regenerative ability. I wouldn't heal instantly, but months of healing and therapy afterwards condensed into a couple of weeks wasn't something to scoff at.

Today wasn't a bad day. Wasn't a great day, but it wasn't a bad day. Bad guys beaten, God pleased, I didn't accidentally pledge myself to a pantheon or accidentally trip my Overdrive beyond level 5, bringing the FBI down on my ass with one of their ever-present snipers and a head-bursting Fragmentation Bullet. I was half a million bucks American richer, and I was even able to stop a vicious cult from starting before it even had a chance to lay hands on a powerful artifact.

And Morrow Kind had made a move, once again, after

Taboo 0: Cliché of Memories
two years of having laid low and off the map.

Things were going to get a helluva lot busier 'round these parts...but that's the way we like it.

Balance in all things, and balance had been kept.

Tomorrow's going to be a good day, one way or another.

****

The Generalist
And now for a preview of
The Generalist – Taboo 1: Where's the Beef?

"...So as you can see, we STILL think that you're the best person around to help us, help our marriage. After all, all who dwell within our circles say so, and you yourself have proven to be a strong empath in the past. Certainly you can help us, Mr. Todd?"

The couple that sat on Frank Todd's couch were beautiful in the same way one could say a sunset was beautiful in the middle of the summer. Each had the ethereal beauty once prized in each of their genders, the female both comely beyond words and yet approachable, her figure both slim and bounteous, her dazzlingly ice-blue eyes flashing both mirth and malice. The male her twin of sorts, both with platinum-blonde hair held long and in extremely complicated braids, save where she was the figure of feminine perfection his slim musculature promised both pleasure as well as violent strength, his eyes a deep, rich forest green in contrast to hers. Beautiful as they were, as slim and clean the lines of their tastefully chosen clothes were, the sharp cream color of her dress and the tanned brown slacks and clean white button-up shirt he wore, the strange combination of fragility and threat they both represented across multiple realms paled in comparison to the sheer amount of frustration that filled the expansive second floor of The Shop.

Taboo 0: Cliché of Memories

For opposite of such perfect beauty lay the source of the rooms' irate frustration and outright fury, the man known as Frank Todd, one of the notorious co-owners of The Shop, a general paranormal good store and special services that lay at the heart of Los Angeles, California. He was Frank Todd: monster slayer and exorcist, mystic and esper, warrior and artificer, hunter and scholar, normally an eccentric and incredibly angry man but at the moment his demeanor lay somewhere between seething and a slow burn.

The Generalist.

Powerful muscles bunched at his shoulders as his broad back and barrel chest were exaggerated by the voluminous, fluffy black bathrobe he wore, de-emphasizing his thick midsection and tree-trunk like thighs, made so through martial arts exertion and daily training. With those legs he had kicked holes through doors, chests, and demons, and at that moment he was seriously considering doing just that to the couple that now took up residence on the couch in his open-plan living space, clutching at each others' hands nervously despite how intensely steady and otherworldly their eyes were.

In his fist, tightly-gripped, was his coffee mug. It was his favorite coffee mug, the handle shaped like a pair of brass knuckles.

The Generalist

It was filled with coffee. Delicious, black, warm coffee fresh from his expensive coffeemaker (one of the few personal luxuries he allowed himself in this realm) that would've been drunk already by now if the couple hadn't appeared on his black leather couch from the time he crossed from the kitchen area to the living room area, intent on his morning book and drink.

"Shut up. Get out," Frank grumped at them, his frown as lumpy and angry as his unpicked afro, his long, straight bangs still stuck to his cheek, "How did you get past my wards? Who the FUCK invited you?!"

"Well, it's like we said, Mr. Todd," the male nodded towards him enthusiastically, his eyes turning bright with hope, "Our marriage hasn't been the same since the mound had to move to Orange County, and seeing as how you DO have a contract with us directly, it's up to you to help us fix this!"

The female looked at him with a banked coolness, one that Frank knew intensely was an illusion - like most of the women he had experienced in this lifetime, they could easily flare to a murderous heat.

One that he was feeling a bit himself the more his coffee cooled.

"Hey boss, got yer mail - did you know your wards are down?" From the other end of the second floor, up a set

Taboo 0: Cliché of Memories

of reinforced stairs lumbered the other partner of The Shop, one of the few known monster-gened people publicly active. Unlike other monster-genes, people who underwent metamorphosis and took on the physical characteristics and abilities of those monstrosities of aeons past who begat their bloodline, the partner lacked the chaotic bloodlust and desire to consume human flesh. Indeed, Daniel "Dash" Hopkins had all his faculties and memories as a human even as he underwent metamorphosis, and while this remained a constant humiliation to him in the beginning he had, through the help of Frank and the establishment of The Shop, come to recognize the strengths his troll heritage gave him. Taller than Frank's modest 5'9" and various shades of green all over, though his trunk looked human enough his humongous clawed hands, feet, and long arms immediately gave away his monster heritage. Though his face was mostly human (outside of the scales visible on his cheeks and chin, the rest scattered about his body and acting as gauntlets and greaves on his shins and forearms), his true blood revealed itself whenever he so much as grinned lightly, his mouth filled with layer after layer of shark-like, sharply jagged teeth. His clothes and boots all had to be custom-made, but as one-half owner of The Shop he had more than enough funds for such a thing.

At the moment, the troll looked up from the collection of mail he was pouring over and blinked at the couple on the couch, "Who the fuck invited YOU?!"

The Generalist

Frank pointed at Dash without looking from the couple, "I know," he swung his large finger at the couple, "Shut up," he then pointed directly at the huge bay window that took up the entire section of the eastern wall, "Get out!"

Oberon, recognized king of the Seelie Sidhe, known to humanity in general throughout the ages as the Fae, frowned darkly at him, "That's not fair, Todd. By the covenant we made with you-"

"Yeah, I know Obie. And I also stipulated that it had to be AFTER breakfast! A breakfast which I haven't even BEGUN to-" Frank motioned to his coffee and then blinked, his chocolate brown eyes puzzled as the liquid slowly sank into the cup without any known leak.

Titania, lowering her slim hand, gave him a smile that had dazzled more than one king in the long annals of human history, "And now your breakfast is done. Will you help us now, Mr. Todd?"

Franks' subsequent roar of sheer rage, incredulous and inarticulate, drove the two to blink out of the physical realm and harms' way even as Dash rushed to calm his partner down.

The Generalist - Taboo 1: Where's the Beef?!
Because you simply cannot read about people getting punched in the face ENOUGH!

CONSUME!

You have many paths to travel, adventurer~! Buy, review, and share to further the conquest of Massive Entertainment!

The Generalist - Taboo 0: Cliché of Memories

Consume for free with a digital download at Smashwords!
https://www.smashwords.com/books/view/239832

Snag a copy from Amazon! Because...Amazon! $1.50 digital download - http://www.amazon.com/The-Generalist-Clich%C3%A9-Memories-ebook/dp/B009F7K5U4

Place your very own physical copy amongst your inventory from Createspace!
https://www.createspace.com/4040960

CONSUME! ONLY THROUGH CONSUMPTION OF MASSIVE QUANTITIES SHALL MY HATRED AND DARKNESS GROW I mean...light and...uh..friendship.

FIGHT THE GOOD FIGHT WITH MASSIVE ENTERTAINMENT!

Made in the USA
San Bernardino, CA
15 January 2014